Lock Down Publications and Ca$h
Presents

PRODUCT OF THE STREETS 2

The Retributions

I0564754

A Novel By
DEMONDE "MONEY" ANDERSON

Lock Down Publications
P.O. Box 944
Stockbridge, GA 30281
www.lockdownpublications.com

Like our page on Facebook: Lock Down Publications
www.facebook.com/lockdownpublications.ldp

Stay Connected with Us!

Text **LOCKDOWN** to 22828 to stay up-to-date with new releases, sneak peaks, contests and more…

Like our page on Facebook:
Lock Down Publications

Join Lock Down Publications/The New Era Reading Group

Visit our website:
www.lockdownpublications.com

Follow us on Instagram:
Lock Down Publications

Email Us: We want to hear from you!

Dedications

In the name of Allah, most gracious, most merciful, I want to dedicate this version of P.O.T.S. to my significant other, my love, my soul. You honestly don't know what you mean to this world in a whole, but through Allah, I plan to show you your true value as a wife and as a strong, beautiful, and highly motivated BLACK WOMAN. I love you and I've watched you evolve. Ma, you are truly a QUEEN.

Also, I dedicate this version of P.O.T.S. to my GHETTO and the struggle and to my neighborhood. All three have helped me and groomed me into having the imagination to see things in this mind of mine that helped shape, form, and create these stories. S/O to my hood, mane! THIRD WARD, STAND UP, FRFR!

Acknowledgements

I wanna give a big shout out to all the people in my life that have pushed me to become the person I am today. To all the people and loved ones that inspired me to keep penning this paper and chasing my dreams, I love y'all!

Demond "Money" Anderson

Chapter 1

Two Months Later

"Mr. Miller!"

Young Mack heard his name being called by the young assistant behind the desk.

He snapped from his daydream as he sat inside the comfortable waiting area along with three others. He'd been waiting patiently for the better half of an hour, listening to them express their darkest problems with one another. Not that he minded them sharing with each other, nor that they were forcing him to listen. The factor that bothered him, which he'd gathered from listening, was the fact that neither of them knew each other in the least bit. There were things that he was dealing with, but he could never imagine himself sharing those things with anyone besides his mother and father. Well, then again, there was someone - a special someone - but the calling of his name interrupted his thoughts of her. He made a mental note to reach out to her soon.

"Yeah, that's me," Young Mack answered, getting the man's attention.

"Ms. Gaines will see you now." The assistant smiled humbly.

Young Mack stood and set the issue of *Black Enterprise* magazine back on the center table where he'd gotten it from. He then followed behind the guy, who escorted him into the back office where Ms. Gaines sat in deep conversation on her office phone.

"Thanks, Jerry. I'll take it from here," she stated, and her assistant disappeared as he came in.

Young Mack noted the warm smile Ms. Gaines wore on her face when addressing her assistant, who seemed at least twice her junior. He smiled with thoughts of the young black guy banging the successful, older white woman. She was sexy though, even in his eyes.

She cleared her throat politely before looking over Young Mack with a warm smile before introducing herself with a tender handshake. "Hi, my name is Miley Gaines. I'm the psychiatric specialist for the facility in which your mother is being treated."

"Nice to meet you, Ms. Gaines," Young Mack said, accepting her hand with a warm smile that matched hers.

"Well, I called you in to discuss with you the matters of your mother's treatment plan. Don't worry though, because this is just a routine visit for families of patients that are responding well to the facility's program." Ms. Gaines took her seat and offered him to do the same.

He watched silently as she opened a folder atop her desk and examined what he knew to be his mother's profile. She remained silent as she studied the notes inside of the folder before speaking.

"Well, Mr. Miller, your mother has been doing quite well and has had a truly magnificent recovery. Her profile is amongst those who have made this place the highest-rated treatment facility in all fifty states." Ms. Gaines smiled and closed the folder before clasping her hands together on top of it.

"That's great news, and I can't express how proud I am of her after hearing that. She was determined to turn her life around and there was nothing I wasn't prepared to provide her with," Young Mack replied honestly.

"Now that's beautiful. The love of a mother's son is a power matched by none other, and I must admit that amount you've shelled over for her treatment was truly appreciated by all of our staff there. We thank you, and with all the success your mom has had working with us, we'd like to provide you two with a three day all-expense paid vacation to the Bahamas Island Resort."

"That's very kind of you and your facility," Young Mack cut her off, "but a vacation for me would be nearly impossible with all that I'm involved in right now. My investments are high profile, and most require my presence around the clock."

"But I'm sure you'd be able to make time to support your mother's successful graduation," she interrupted him this time.

He could clearly see that this was a woman that was used to having things her way. One thing he was sure of was that she'd never encountered anyone like him with all the weight he was carrying on his shoulders, so he excused her interruption and stared deeply into her eyes. He truly hadn't noticed her ice blue eyes until that very moment, and the way she demanded his attention with her appeal was like nothing he'd been around in all of his young years. Her gaze was sensual, her demeanor was something other, and he was getting aroused by the older woman.

"Look, Ms. Gaines, I understand everything you're tryna say with your last statement and yes, I will always make time for my mother no matter what's going on in my life, but I am a businessman. Three days outta reach would be hard on my company, and my clients aren't your average investors. They'd die and come back to haunt me if I pulled something like that. Business is very important to my family, and with the way things are, I'm the only one available to run the day-to-day operations." Young Mack did his best to present himself as the professional he proclaimed to be when he enrolled his mother into their facility.

Ms. Gaines was moved by the power exuding from the young, handsome, and sexy man before her. Unbeknownst to Young Mack, she was well aware of his family's history. She'd done her research on their family, and the story about his father and their family attracted her to them like a moth to a flame. She'd never worked so close with a woman of Sylvia's caliber with a past so extensive. Seeing Sylvia when she first arrived there with them was like seeing the living corpse of her old self. Sylvia's turnaround was one for the books. Their sessions were powerful and heartfelt, and Ms. Gaines couldn't understand for the life of her how these people had won her infatuation. Maybe it was his father...no, it was definitely his mother. Hell, she was lost in a field she had dominated for the better half of her life. Sitting across from him now had her even more confused than she already was. He was young like she loved her conquests. He was strong both mentally and what looked to be physically. Handsome like his father, strongly appealing, and both intelligent and mysterious like his mother. His presence made her center melt.

"I understand, Mr. Miller, but there must be a definite way that I can thank you for your generous contribution," she stated while removing her glasses and releasing her ponytail.

Her hair was blonde, past her shoulders, and the smile she now wore very much exposed her intentions. Young Mack was sure she meant exactly what he thought she meant as the bulge in his dress pants became very visible.

"I mean, there are other ways." He smiled, feeding into her seduction.

"Should I lock the door?" she asked, loving the threat of someone walking in on them.

"Not if you hurry," Young Mack stated with charm as he stood and released his Jimmy Choo belt buckle.

"My pleasure," Ms. Gaines moaned as she came around her desk and got to her knees between his legs.

9

***

Aeriella must have checked herself in the mirror over a hundred times as she readied herself to represent her newest client for the first time. Things were different for her this time around. She had never represented anyone she cared for in the way she cared for this client. His case was one that she had studied from a great distance for many years, and to be this close and personal in the appeals procedure made her more than a little nervous.

"Hey mija, esta bien?" Marie questioned her daughter after peeping her head inside of her bedroom.

It had been years since Aeriella actually stayed home with her mother and father. Together, they really missed their daughter staying at home with them, so much so that they never touched her childhood bedroom besides the usual dusting and swapping bed dressings. Having her back there now was nothing short of a blessing to her parents.

"Hey Ma," Aeriella turned and greeted her mother. "I'm good, just tryna look the part for this new case."

"Honey, you look great." Maria laughed while stepping into the room and moving behind her daughter.

"Think so?"

"Of course, mija. You nearly are as perfect as your mother." They shared a laugh at her mother's sense of humor.

Maria was indeed a beautiful woman. She was a well-proportioned Hispanic woman and men drooled over her everywhere. Aeriella was definitely her mother reincarnated.

"Thanks, Ma, because you really are perfect." Aeriella Aeriella put her left hand atop her mother's left hand as it rested on her shoulder.

"Ahh, Aeriella, are you trying to make your mother cry?" a deep voice came in from the room's doorway.

"Hi Dad," Aeriella spoke to her father, looking at him through the mirror before her.

10

"'Sup, baby girl." Kevin inched his head up at his daughter.

"Hey love, how are you this morning?" Maria greeted her husband of a lifetime.

"I'm good, especially after seeing my ladies spending quality time together."

Maria kissed her hand and blew him a kiss through the mirror that he caught and placed over his heart. Their love was powerful and they never went a day without expressing it to one another. Aeriella loved and admired her parents' marriage and friendship. They were inseparable, and she longed for a love strong enough to fit into the same book as her parents and Young Mack's parents. As dysfunctional as they were at the time, their love was immeasurable on any scale.

Thinking of Young Mack's parents, Aeriella kissed her mother, then moved to the bed where her suit jacket was. After getting herself together, she grabbed her designer briefcase, stepped to her father, and kissed him the same as she had her mother. He wrapped her up in his masculine arms before kissing her forehead the way he always did before she stepped foot outside of the house.

"I'm proud of the strong and positive woman you've become," her father said, hugging her tightly.

"So, you're getting your lick back?" Aeriella playfully asked her father.

"What'chu mean getting my lick back?" Kevin asked, looking her deep into her honey brown eyes.

"You asked earlier if I were tryna make Ma cry, and now you stand here trying to make me cry." All three shared a good laugh at that revelation.

"I love you and I'm glad you're back with us for as long as you feel you need to be," he said and then kissed her forehead again.

"Could be permanently," Maria suggested.

"You tried it, Ma!" Aeriella laughed at her mother's steady attempt to get her to move back in. "I'm grown now and you two need your space and privacy, especially after last night."

Maria cupped her hands over her mouth, embarrassed that her daughter had heard their passionate lovemaking last night. Keven laughed heartily after hearing that, but he wasn't the least bit embarrassed because he was proud to still be able to satisfy his sweet wife passionately in bed.

"Uh-uh, I gotta get outta here and get to work," Aeriella said after stepping outta her father's embrace.

"Okay, baby. We'll prepare ahead of time for yet another victory for our amazing lawyer of a daughter," Maria stated as Aeriella left them holding each other in the doorway.

"Thanks. I'll be home later, so save dinner for me," she said over her shoulder.

"Home sounds real good, mija!" Maria replied as her daughter climbed inside of her vehicle and waved as she drove away.

Aeriella was all smiles while entering the federal courthouse in downtown Houston. Young Mack had called on her way over and informed her that he would be arriving shortly to support her and his father. She couldn't wait to see him again.

The courthouse was unusually crowded once she stepped through its doors. The noise decreased and everyone looked in her direction as she strutted to a section labeled with her name on it. The table was outfitted with a pitcher of water and a glass already filled. There was a pen and a legal tablet there as well. She smiled at the generous gesture that she knew was put there by the District Attorney, but he wasn't dealing with an amateur by a long shot.

After collecting those things from her table, she kindly walked them over to the DA's table and set them there while every person in attendance watched her. She didn't say a word as she made her way back to her table and removed her personal stationery things. She then stepped to the DA and smiled while extending her hand in greetings.

"Hi, my name is Aeriella Garcia, and I'm here to represent——"

"Mackentosh Miller, yeah, I know." The crude look on his face expressed his distaste in her being there for that very reason.

"Ms. Garcia, I hope you understand the level of criminal you are here to try and set free," the DA went on talking without shaking her hand.

"Yes, I do understand the level of criminal I'm dealing with, and let's hope for your sake and for the sake of the federal courts that I'm indeed representing the aforementioned criminal and you're not. But we could always cut the bull and send my client home to be with his family and save the courts the embarrassment of going the distance with this." Aeriella made herself clear. She was fully aware of all the traps and illegal means the federal agencies used to lock her client away, and she intended to expose every single one for the judge to see for himself.

***

Mackmillions was dressed to the nines as he positioned himself to be cuffed and shackled for court. He'd grown used to the procedure after being confined for so many years. The officers handled him as high risk same as every institution he had ever been in since his incarceration. It had been over a decade since he'd been back in the great city of Houston, and the view of downtown nearly stole his breath away. This was a city he once ruled over in the underworld since he was a savage teenaged boy, and the air welcomed him back home when he stepped off the fully bulletproof truck he had been transported in. He smiled at the very essence of the wind blowing against his skin and coursing its way through his nostrils. He hadn't felt a sensation so intense since he married his wife and she birthed their child. Being back made him think of his past, the people he'd lost to the life or behind bars for sticking up for him during his fall from the throne. He missed them dearly. Being back here also make him miss his wife desperately. He wondered about her so much, but chose not to inquire about her. He chose to keep her tucked away inside of his heart, where she would live even after life. She was his life no matter how much life changed on them. Sylvia was his and he was hers.

The singsong sound of the elevator reaching its destination shook him from his intense feelings of being back at home. The door opened and they were met by two more armed guards with real mean looks on their faces. He silently wondered which one of his old acquaintances in higher places had been behind hiring so much security for this procedure. Together the four armed guards handled his escort until they made it to the courtroom where his lawyer and others were awaiting his arrival. Three of the armed guards set up stations around the entrance of the courtroom while one held tight to his arm and continued through the double doors, where he first laid eyes on the huge turnout for his case. It wasn't a surprise to him though because he knew what this could mean for a lot of parties involved in his entrapment. He smiled at all the crooked politicians and their henchmen as he walked past them and past his young, beautiful attorney. He nodded his head in approval as the armed guard escorted him to the secluded section directly across from the jury box. He stepped inside as the guard instructed before the door was slammed shut.

Aeriella quickly approached the judge and demanded her client be seated next to her during the proceedings, but was quickly shot down by the judge.

"That won't be possible, Ms. Garcia. Now make your way back over there and ask for permission before you approach me again."

Aeriella nodded her understanding before heading back to her table.

"Can we now proceed?" the judge asked as the DA shuffled through paperwork.

"Of course, Your Honor," the smug district attorney stated, trying to hide the fact that he laughed at Aeriella's attempt to get the judge to seat Miller next to her. She clearly didn't understand the high risk her client was to everyone in the room.

Aeriella hated his guts. The arrogant kiss-ass moved around like he ran the world.

"Your Honor, this case is in the matter of Mackentosh Miller, a well-known drug kingpin, ruthless killer, extortionist, and money launderer. He was the youngest known crime lord of Houston's notorious underworld, but by far the wealthiest to ever be detained by the Federal Bureau of Investigation."

Aeriella listened intently for nearly an entire hour as the district attorney went about accusing Mr. Mackmillions of every known crime one could commit against the law. None of it fazed her, because it was their opinion and they were entitled to that. She was okay with him doing him because none of what he was presenting now had not already been presented, which meant there was nothing new working in their favor.

"Mr. Shavers, I'm well aware of these matters and with all due respect, I've heard it and read it enough times not to want to hear it again. Is there by chance anything new you would like to add to this case before we give Ms. Garcia a chance to plead her case?" the judge asked, turning the tanned skin on the district attorney's face red.

"No, Your Honor, there is nothing new. I was just stating the facts acquired by years of federal investigations and countless hours spent by our cohorts to convict Mr. Miller."

"Well, the court thanks you for your fine presentation, but we've heard it and dreadfully read it over and over again."

ᴚ towards Mr. Mackmillions after hearing ᴊniss the DA's presentation. He smiled slightly .ᴇ her a nod towards the judge.

"Now Ms. Garcia, I pray that you have something worthy of our attention, because I would hate to have to sit through yet another round of this case's past findings."

"Yes, Your Honor, I completely understand. I was beginning to grow a bit fatigued myself."

"Well, let's hear it."

"To be truthful, Your Honor, there isn't much I would like to expose to the court's public opinion," Aeriella stated while gathering her paperwork to present to the judge.

"Ha!" the DA chuckled at the antics of his opponent.

"Excuse me, but you can't really be serious right now," the judge stated, clearly disappointed.

"Yes, in fact, I am, Your Honor. With all the high-profile individuals stated in this packet in attendance here along with the extraordinary attention this case has received from the media giants around the world, one would only wish to keep our findings and tremendous errors of the federal agencies in confidential safeguard of your eyes only. if that's okay with you Your Honor."

"Objection! She can't possibly be granted that we keep a closed eye in this situation!" DA Shavers jumped out of his seat.

"Overruled! Mr. Shavers, you are aware that this is not yet a trial proceeding, right?"

After careful consideration from the judge in the matter of granting Aeriella's request, the judge permitted her to approach the bench with her packet.

"Ms. Garcia, you do realize that this is a very unorthodox manner you are bringing forth in this courtroom?"

"Yes, Your Honor I'm aware of that, but for the security of this case, I know it is a well-needed one. That is, until you are ready to proceed and expose this poorly-handled case for what it is." Aeriella stood firm on her decision.

"Quiet down!" the judge ordered with a bang of his gavel.

Murmurs could be heard everywhere after Aeriella made her last attempt.

"I would like to assure you that as guilty as they made my client seem, he was indeed railroaded and wrongly convicted in his trial." Aeriella poured her sauce on thick.

"Everything you have stated here this evening has been duly noted and recorded, Ms. Garcia."

"You can't possibly be serious!" DA Shavers yelled out.

"One more outburst from you, Mr. Shavers, and this evening will be your last one in federal court. Do I make myself absolutely clear?"

"Yes, Your Honor," DA Shavers replied, sitting back in defeat.

"Now if the government rests upon all evidence heard in this case matter, we will proceed once Ms. Garcia's filing is reviewed. So, is that all, DA Shavers?"

"Yes, Your Honor. This is crazy," the cowardly attorney stated under his breath.

"Is there something you would like to say to the court?" the judge asked Mr. Shavers about his incoherent mumbling.

"No, nothing at all."

"What about you, Ms. Garcia? Is there anything you would like to add?" the judge questioned.

"Well, there is just one other thing, Your Honor."

Chapter 2

Young Mack couldn't believe how exhausted he was after leaving Miley's office. She was indeed a wild woman on a mission. Sex was incredible with her, and it turned out that he truly enjoyed her wet and warm treasure. Her throat game was to die for and she had little to no gag reflex, taking his iron like the true pro she was. Just thinking about their sexual exploits in her office had his shit on brick as he yawned and slammed his hand down on his alarm clock. He sat up in bed and stretched his muscular arms above his head. He grabbed his aching package and smiled to himself.

I gotta hit that gym, he thought to himself. "That demon could never be classified as a cougar," he said out loud with a chuckle before standing from his bed, removing his Versace boxer briefs, and walking into his bathroom.

Hot water splashed against his head and body from all sides as he leaned against the glass shower wall, trying his best to shake the grogginess. Steam rose from the heat of the water misting the floor to ceiling glass encasing him. It was exactly what he needed. His stress levels were high, and after missing his father's court appearance, he was pissed with himself for spending so much time in Miley's office. But for some strange reason, he didn't fault his actions, because Miley was a bad bitch on all levels. He was young, and her temptations roared loud like a feline in heat. There was no way he could resist the tremendous urge to get inside of her.

After he showered and took care of his hygiene, he walked to the nightstand next to his king-sized bed and collected his phones. Young Mack was a busy man after acquiring a new shipment of drugs from his coke connections. Things were quite calm in the streets and money was pouring in hand over fist. He couldn't complain in the least bit. Two of his phones showed that he had over twenty missed calls and just as many unread text messages. He read through every one of them, responding to the necessary ones while making calls to his men in response to the business at his trap houses. It was early in the a.m., and even though he wasn't a morning person, the last few months had accustomed him to it. Business was booming and there was nothing he loved more in the game than raking it in.

He concluded the transactions on his business lines before looking over the unread messages on his third phone. There was one from Ambrea and another from Aeriella, the two main women in his life. His bond with Aeriella was growing as strong as it was when they were younger and deeply in love. Young Mack had been her first love and she was his and together, they were each other's first everything.

His relationship with Ambrea was extremely complicated for the both of them. She stood at 5'5" and weighed a healthy 125 pounds. Her hair was naturally red, inherited through her English grandmother, and it hung past her shoulders and stopped at her lower back. She was extremely sexual and lived in the gym, so it was safe to say that she was stacked in all the right places. She had six pack abs, a slim waist, protruding hips with thick thighs, and an ass made truly from every man's dream. She was banging like that and some. Honestly, both women were killing shit and stood neck and neck in the dime race. He'd never be able to choose who was baddest, but he shared a deeper connection and was certainly more drawn to Aeriella.

Ambrea's message was short and sweet. She'd wished him good luck and asked him to stay safe and ended her message with three heart emojis. He was connected to her in more ways than one. She was the twin sister to his close friend Ashton. Surely Ashton knew that his sister and friend crushed on one another but for years now, Ashton never knew that they were actually sleeping together. Young Mack and Ambrea felt mutual about keeping their relationship a secret, mostly due to Ambrea being the fiancée of Young Mack's coke connect, Señor Gurdo. Gurdo, or Fatboy, came from a prominent cartel background dating back to as far as the early 1950s. Gurdo was crowned head of his family once his father retired and the world now recognized him as Señor Gurdo. He was madly in love with Ambrea and if he ever discovered their betrayal, there was no question as to what the drug lord would do. So as dangerous as it was, they vowed to keep their thing exactly that: their thing.

He sent her a thumbs up emoji before opening and reading Aeriella's message. What he read almost burst his heart. His eyes grew to the size of saucers and his pulse raced so fast that he thought he was about to have a heart attack. He slammed his back against his memory foam mattress and yelled in joy.

"Yesssss!"

He jumped up and hurried inside of his closet. He'd upgraded his living after warring with one of his father's oldest rivals. Shit was going good with his drug business now that Phatts was dead and with the money he was raking in, he splurged on not just himself, but all of his top lieutenants. He now lived in a high rise hidden deep in the heart of downtown Houston. It was a fifty-five hundred square feet with five bedrooms and three baths, a huge entertainment room, sauna, multi-leveled living room, and indoor hot tub. The pad was huge and laced and was worth more than Young Mack cared to share with anyone besides his broker. It was comfortable for him and his three-man live-in security team. He rushed to dress his naked frame in original Gucci print boxer briefs, an Adidas track suit with matching gray over white Adidas superstars. He couldn't believe the news Aeriella had dropped on him, and he was almost late to the twelve o'clock meeting with one of his father's old friends in which she requested his presence 911.

After alerting his men of his need to depart, he selected the head of his security detail to travel with him while the other two, which were blood brothers, remained behind and held his home down.

"Josh, Pop's on the way home, kid!" Young Mack exclaimed as they jumped into his AMG G 63 Benz truck.

It was no surprise to Young Mack that Joshua remained silent as he released his excitement. Josh was a certified workaholic and took his job with vital seriousness. While out and about, Young Mack's safety was always his first and main concern. Nothing else mattered. He'd kill and dismember anything and anyone that possibly pose a threat to Young Mack or his crew. He remained stone-faced as he gave Young Mack a head nod before positioning his earpiece behind then inside of his ear. He checked to see if Sham and Tree could hear him and after receiving confirmation, he focused on the road as Young Mack drove to their destination. Minutes later, Young Mack parked his truck at the front door of a weather-worn trailer home surrounded by over an acre of lush green land. After stepping out of his ride, he heard a horse neigh in the distance. Young Mack wasn't sure who lived at this address, but he checked his messages again to be sure it was indeed the right one.

"This is it, but I don't see Aeriella's whip anywhere," Young Mack stated, looking all around them. The area was calm all around and he could surely feel the serenity of being out there.

"Someone is inside," Josh stated after witnessing the blinds in the window move.

"It's cool, J. At least they know we're out here. But until we know why we're here, let's mob easy and wait for Aeriella," Young Mack said while checking his Rolly for the time. Aeriella was running late, and that wasn't like her at all. He checked his last text message and decided to call her.

"I'm almost there," Aeriella stated once she answered.

"Almost here…" Young Mack's voice trailed off as he locked eyes with the crazed-looking man moving stealthily towards them with an assault rifle leading the way. Josh slowly moved in front of Young Mack with his arms in the air to show the man that they came in peace.

"Young Mack, are you okay?" Aeriella's voice sounded as Young Mack held his hands in the air as well.

"We don't want no trouble, old timer," Josh stated, already steaming from the guy having the ups on them.

"Dat's wat dem say too," Max growled, motioning his head towards the two wooden axes positioned next to each other.

Dirt was piled in two heaps underneath a huge tree, and Young Mack knew those were indeed burial grounds for the people Max was referring to.

Aeriella's car pulled up swiftly and parked behind Young Mack's truck. She moved with haste after hearing the drama over Young Mack's phone.

"Max!" Everyone heard her voice, but no one turned to look in her direction. "Everything is as it should be, Max!" Aeriella mouthed the exact words Mr. Mackmillions had ordered her to.

"Who you?" Max questioned seriously. He knew those words without a shadow of a doubt, but what was her relation to their source?

"Mackmillions wanted me to ask you if he has ever let you down before?"

"Little gurl, you know not what you speak to me right now." Max gritted his teeth as he stared at the two men before him.

"He's your nephew, Max. That's Young Mack, Mackmillions's son. You don't wanna hurt him," Aeriella pleaded.

"Nawl, keep your eyes on me, homeboy. She's no threat to you, and neither are we," Young Mack finally spoke up once Max's eyes traveled over to Aeriella.

Bringing Max's attention back to him, he stepped out from behind Josh's body. The two men stared each other in the eyes in silence as Josh and Aeriella looked on.

"I heard her call you Max. Am I right?" Max nodded as he listened to Young Mack without saying a word.

"You were my father's best friend and right-hand man, right? Maxmillion, that's what he used to call you as you rained hell through the lives and hearts of anyone that stood in the way of you and my father, am I right?" Young Mack thought back to a time when his father would tell him all about him and Max running through the city tearing shit up.

Max's expression never wavered as he studied Young Mack, observing how much he really did look like his closest comrade. Living life in the streets alongside Mackmillions was nothing short of a pleasure and a gift to anyone who had been blessed to live after doing so. Max didn't get any visitors unless someone else had come to take his life away and erase him from the face of the earth. He hated the attention, but he loved the thrill of his kills.

"So you really me neph, ya?" Max asked as he lowered his murder weapon.

"Yeah, it's me, Max," Young Mack exhaled.

"Full grown nah. You look good, boi. How de ol' man?"

"He's fine, Max and he's coming home. He wants you to be there when he's released and he told me to tell you it's time," Aeriella said.

"He say dat?" Max couldn't believe his ears. Mackmillions told him this day would come and now that it had, he could feel the monster yawning inside of him. Aeriella confirmed with a head nod.

"Wait 'ere," Max stated before disappearing inside of the trailer home.

"Glad you could make it." Young Mack looked at Aeriella and sarcastically wiped sweat from his brow.

"Just following orders." She smiled.

Young Mack looked at her skeptically after that statement. "You used me as bait?" He could read right through her.

"No, not me. Your father. He knew you were the only familiar face that could get through to Max. Otherwise, no matter what I told him, your father said he would surely kill me - or anyone else, for that matter."

Before Young Mack could gather his thoughts and reply, Max came out of the trailer home with three black duffle bags, one on his shoulder and the other two in his hands.

"Let's go!" he stated in his deep Creole accent.

***

It had been months since Mary lost her loving husband and she could still feel the decimating anguish of her loss. It seemed like the more time passed, the harder it was for her to accept the reality of her situation. Losing him was torturing to her soul and by far the worst pain next to losing her son to the streets. She'd lost her son to the system by the hands and fuckery of her own mother. Having her son back after so many years brought forth a happiness on a level that she just couldn't explain with words. She'd missed him desperately his entire life, and so much time had passed without them getting to know each other. To have him back now all grown up sometimes toyed with her heart.

Just when she thought there could be peace after so much destruction in her life, her whole world got twisted inside of a cyclone, and now there was numbness all over. Losing a son and a husband would probably kill a normal wife day by day until she took her own life but now, after finding her long lost son the same day she lost her husband, it gave her something else to fight for. Today was Mary's day and she was doing her best to stay occupied as she shopped throughout the Galleria Mall.

Stepping out of Mui Mui's designer store, her phone vibrated in her hand. Looking at the screen, she sighed in frustration before picking up.

"Hello?" the deep voice spoke after she answered without saying anything.

"I'm listening," Mary stated dryly.

"When will you decide to make time, Mary?"

It had been a while since she'd heard a word from Kenndrick. KenKen, as everyone called him, had recently been blowing her up about some type of business - business that was, of course, her late husband's problem and glory. She could never understand how men loved anything other than money while hustling in the streets. Fuck the thrill. All she needed was the bills, and her husband Phatts did stack them. Losing him after losing their son left her with a burning rage, a rage so strong that it could only be neutralized by revenge.

"Listen, KenKen, I told you that I would contact you when and if business needs to progress, but until then, my husband made sure that me and our child would want for nothing in his absence, so for now we're straight," Mary stated much to KenKen's dismay.

"Mary, I've known you for so many years I couldn't begin to count them, but never have I taken you to be this naïve. There is no such thing as when or even if business will progress in this game. Your husband was a power player and a real close friend of mine. We're both wealthy and powerful men, and if for a second you think that your husband and I are on the level that we are by fucking with people that are under and beneath us, then Mary, I'm sorry to tell you that you're sadly mistaken, and I fear that your life and the life of that son that never got to know his father is in grave danger. Someone has to replace his seat at the round table, and it's his death right that someone from his immediate family take that seat before it is offered to anyone else." KenKen was seriously trying his best to get through to her.

"So let someone else take the damn seat then," Mary stated, sick off the entire situation.

"That someone else would then have to erase you and your child to completely be accepted by the others at the table to be sure that there will be no loose ends that could possibly come back to haunt them," KenKen confessed.

Mary didn't have the words to respond to all that he was exposing her to so quickly. She cared nothing about this so-called realm her husband had gotten involved with. His dealings had nothing to do with her, and he made sure to keep her outside of nearly all of his dealings in the streets. Hell, she lost a son to the streets in part because of something her husband had done. She'd been shot by a man that they later found out was her long-lost son who was on a rampage to kill her husband his father. So as far as she could see it, those people could kiss her natural black ass.

"These people won't stay quiet for long. Mary, I'll do my best to buy you as much time as I can. You have my number if you need anything. I owe it to Phatts to make sure that you and your son have the best chance, and I intend to do just that," KenKen stated before hanging up.

She spent the rest of her evening shopping, in deep thought of her conversation with KenKen. She couldn't tell if the man was just being persistent about doing business, or if his words should be taken seriously. She wasn't aware of how deep her husband was in the streets and if KenKen could be trusted, so she decided to get her shopping out of the way before she made her final decision on it. On her way out of the mall, her phone vibrated, showcasing her son's face.

"How are you?" she answered politely.

"I'm good, Ma, how about you?" He smiled and she could see the joy in his eyes.

"I'm good now, and I'm happy to hear from you." She hated when they went days without talking or seeing each other.

"Same here, beautiful. Well, I was thinking about you and me spending time together to make up for my absence. What do you think about dinner at the house, say around eight?" Rob asked curiously. He had a surprise for her and hoped she would agree to dinner.

"Sure thing, my love, I'll be there. Oh wait, I live there!" They both laughed.

Chapter 3

Eight o'clock had come and gone and Rob was pissed. He'd taken advantage of his mother's kitchen, putting his heart and soul into their meal for the night. He made a succulent pot roast with four cheese scalloped potatoes made from scratch with fresh Idaho potatoes, steamed white rice kissed with garlic butter and topped with shredded cheese. He also threw together one of his favorites, green bean casserole, and baked a pan of sweet fluffy yellow cornbread. Cooking was his thing, and for his T-lady, he was certainly on his best shit with the flavoring and texture of the full course meal.

Anticipation turned into frustration after sitting around waiting for her to return home. He couldn't believe he'd been stood up by the woman that birthed him and for the first time, he could really say that he was disappointed with her. An hour after clearing the table and getting everything situated inside of plastic containers and placed in the fridge, he heard the purring sound of his mother's Maserati Levante SUV pull into the driveway, and seconds later, he heard the garage door close. He shook his head at how late she was and continued doing what he was doing.

Entering her kitchen from the garage, Mary could see the hurt and disappointment in her son's face and his body language told a tale of its own also. She'd missed their dinner night and hated herself for it, but a matter too important to ignore arose and it took more time and sacrifice than she would care to admit.

"Robert, we need to talk," Mary stated after tossing her keys on the marble countertop.

"Maybe tomorrow, 'cause I got somewhere to be. Food is in the fridge in case you get hungry, but I'm sure you've already eaten."

She could tell he was lying about needing to be some place and was definitely gonna call him out on it later but right now, there was no time to be acting like his stubborn late father.

"I know you're upset 'bout me missing our dinner and you know I wouldn't miss that for anything, but what we need to talk about can't wait until tomorrow because it may never come if we don't act now."

Her revelation tugged at his gangsta, and he quickly became protective.

"Your next move will be very vital to you and your mother's existence," KenKen's voice sounded as he stepped into the kitchen behind Mary.

"You threatening us, nigga?" Rob mugged the unknown man while whipping out his favorite S&W .40 filled with blue tip bullets.

KenKen instantly put his hands in the air, seeing that the young man misunderstood his presence.

"We're on the same team."

Mary knew her son was a shooter and had witnessed his work firsthand the night he came to kill his father and took out Skooby, his father's right hand.

"He's not the enemy, son."

"And he damn sho ain't the home team if only our lives are on the line and not his. I'm from the jungle, homeboy, and I know all types of snakes except the kind that don't bite so state yo' intentions, because yo' next words can be vital to your existence." Rob wasn't about to play no games with the man no matter his mother's opinion of him. He didn't know him, so he wasn't shit to him.

"First and foremost, I'm KenKen. Your father and I have been loyal friends damn near our whole lives."

Rob looked at the man skeptically after hearing the most misused word in the English language come outta his mouth. The diamond-encrusted 1975 Royal Oak A series Audemers Peugeot along with a few other pieces of fine jewelry told him that this man was one of wealth. The overly-expensive tailored Kiton dress suit fit his body to perfection and gave away any chances of someone suspecting him to be a novice in the game.

"Loyalty is a very trivial word in this life, KenKen," Rob stated firmly, but he calmed his suspicions of the dude and lowered his weapon.

"Not in my days," KenKen replied as he took a seat at the kitchen island. "Loyal enough to let him marry my sister and not knock his head off for deflowering her," he added while looking to Mary, who just shook her head.

"You never let him live that down either," Mary said with a reminiscent expression.

"Listen, young'un, I won't hold you up for long now that I've brought your mother up on game. I truly feel that this matter should be discussed between the two of you, but being that y'all are family, I gotta explain to you the severity of it all."

"Severity?" Rob asked, fully alerting his eyes in Mary's direction.

"Yes! Unbeknownst to you and your mother, your father was a powerful man in a position he never really got around to care for, nor did he care to understand it either. I've been trying for so long to get him to fulfill his obligations to the Realm, but even though we were chairmen, your father looked at the entire existence of the shared round table as a joke. He didn't believe such power could be shared between friends and foes all in one. He was always a solo act, and by the time the Realm came to recruit him, he merely agreed outta good faith to myself and our late partner Isaac. The Realm is nothing to take lightly, especially for the ones that know we exist, and we've grown stronger than ever through the aid and assistance of our political connections in over twenty states around America. The heart of the Realm's success comes from the moves made in the underworld and like every other organization, drugs are our strong point."

"Drugs? Shiiid, I don't know nothing about drugs," Rob intervened.

"Doesn't matter. After one of you two decide whose gonna be fulfilling your father's obligations to the Realm, it'll be left up to me to be sure that all else falls into place, so don't sweat what you can't control. Learn the lay of the land and control what you can and ask no questions about what you can't," KenKen stated after clasping his fingers together. "The important thing is that the Realm has to fill your father's seat at the round table. There are no exceptions to the fact that if neither you nor your mother takes that seat, someone else will, and for them to be fully accepted into the Realm, they will be ordered to erase your father's bloodline. Meaning the both of you and any grandkids and so forth."

"Fuck outta here with that shit." Rob waved his hand at the man talking outside of his neck. "You talking on some ole make believe cult type shit, bruh."

"Robert, listen to him, please, son, this is not a joke. I didn't wanna believe it either, but after witnessing what I've witnessed today, it makes more sense than not," Mary said, looking her son in the eyes with sincerity.

"Okay, let's say these so-called people send someone to collect on me and my mother's skulls and fail. What then?" He wasn't feeling the pressure coming from this so-called Realm, and the more KenKen explained it, the more he fueled the fire in Rob's gut.

"I just told you someone must fill that seat, so it won't end no matter how triumphant you two are. It will never end

31

unless either of you take that seat or someone takes you out," KenKen promised. "Anywho, I'll leave you two to it. Mary has my personal number. Once the decision is made, use it."

With that being said, KenKen murked out as quietly as he came.

The silence left behind was a thick one as reality kicked the idea that their life could definitely be in the balance of preservation or extermination.

"If you won't take it, I'll have no choice but to."

Rob lifted his head from the palms of his hands and stared at his mother as if she had two heads. "You buying into this hoopla?"

"It's real. I don't have not one doubt in my mind that those people won't hunt us down and kill us. We don't have an army laying in wait for something like this, son. I knew your father was deep in the game, but I never not once got in his business when it came to his dealings, and after witnessing what I did this evening, I know why I never did."

Rob could see the terror through the mirror portals of her soul, and it pained him that whatever she went through today, he wasn't there to care for her.

"So, we're supposed to just play puppet and allow them to pull our strings."

"Taking the seat won't be playing puppet, son, because that seat allows us to create and dictate our own destiny. Did you hear how KenKen said that your father never wanted anything to do with it, and yet he was able to be a member and do his own thing without them anyway? That's how we'll outsmart them. If we do it carefully and execute strategically, we'll leave their door wide open for someone else of our picking to walk right in and take them down."

There was another silence between them, but this time Rob's thoughts were on the fact that his mother wasn't even a street chick, and yet she had the game of a street veteran. He liked the idea of a takeover. Hell, to be honest, he was broke besides the things his mother gave him that belonged to his father. Only thing he'd been engrossed in lately was keeping close tabs on Young Mack and his growing operation. Thinking of his former friend set his blood a boil. He still hadn't gotten down to the bottom of what Young Mack had to do with his father's death, but he was sure of one thing, and that was that Young Mack did have something to do with the situation. Not to mention the rumor spilling about Young Mack and his team dealing death to a brother he never knew he had.

"What's on your mind, Robert?" Mary questioned while rising from her seat to grab something to drink and offering him something as well.

He kindly declined before standing and wrapping her up in his strong arms.

"I'll do it, Ma, but where do we go from here?"

"It'll be tough in the beginning, son, but we'll do fine. I just know we will," Mary stated before getting KenKen on the line.

"Yeah," KenKen answered with his lungs filled with exotic smoke.

"It's a go. He accepts."

"I'm outside."

$$$$$

"That's checkmate in three."

The murky silence of Mackmillions' cell was to be expected when a game of chess was underway. He'd grown a love for the game, and no matter the status of his opponent, he loved to play. A virtuous game of war taught him something every single game he played.

"Nice move, but it was premature, Bonez. Countercheck and mate on my next move," Mackmillions revealed as he positioned his bishop to be taken by Bonez's queen.

"Damn, Mack, that was smooth." Bonez laughed, breaking the silent spell in the small cell.

Everyone had crowded around to watch the absolute best two players thug it out on the chessboard.

"Salute, young gunna, but that's five to two right there," Mackmillions teased.

"Aww shit." Bonez knew that with him losing the match, he would have to honor his duties and cook a meal fit for a prison king - that king being Mr. Mackmillions.

"Nawl, not you, Bonez?" Mack raised his left eyebrow with a shook look on his face.

"You're right, big homie, I own that shit. Good game though, Mack. Now I can't wait to see how you put it down in them streets this go round," Bonez stated as he got up and exited Mackmillions' cell followed by all the spectators.

Bonez didn't realize it, but his words stuck to Mackmillions' mental like he'd glued them there. Mackmillions silently observed the checkmate he'd pinned Bonez into. The youngsta had a way with attacking like he'd never experienced on the board before but like most people who played the game without studying their strongest pieces, he thought Mack's sacrifice of his queen would ultimately win him the game. It was merely a ploy to get Bonez to stack his queen in front of his king so that Mack could trap it with his bishop, which would ultimately cost Bonez the game once Mack sent his rook to the bottom line in line with Bonez's king, who was trapped by Mack's other rook on the top line.

As Bonez's words reverberated throughout his thoughts, Mack couldn't help but to think of what his next move would be. Going home seemed surreal, but he already knew the day would come that his enemies would have to feel his wrath. He also knew he'd have to erase every opposition that stood against him in his court case in order to remain a free man. People in high places had betrayed him, and after all he'd sacrificed to remain loyal to them, after all he'd done for them, he couldn't allow for their transgressions to go unpunished. The thoughts of such treachery raised his temperature and spiked his heart rate, then he thought about everything that Ramone had taught him about mastering himself. He closed his eyes and visions of his wife and son immediately filled the room, putting him in a calmed state and helping to regulate his entire being. A smile slowly spread across his face at the thought of Sylvia. That woman truly did something to his gangsta back in the day and somehow still held that effect on him even after not seeing her in over a decade. "Love" he mouthed to her in his vision and shook his head at her angelic smiling face. After opening his eyes, he couldn't picture running his kingdom without his queen.

Moments later, he sat at a long table enjoying what he hoped would be his last and final prison meal. Bonez had blessed it, and Mackmillions smiled at the youngsta. He saw so much potential in Bonez if he had the right type of push in the right types of directions. He couldn't have been but a year or two older than Young Mack and knew together they'd be a force to be reckoned with. An hour after their meal, everyone heard it over the P.A. system. It was time for Mackmillions to be released, and they gathered to bid the street king their farewells.

"Treat it like the real deal, OG." Bonez shook his hand and accepted the half-hug from someone he could definitely see himself shadowing in the streets.

"As long as I've been away? Shiiid, this is the real deal for me, Bonezy!"

They all laughed at that.

"True shit, true shit. I know you'll beat 'em from the outside. big homie. I get out in a few months, so look me up. If I'm welcomed to sit amongst greatness, I do learn fast."

"Say less. You're already remembered here." Mackmillions pointed to his temple. "That's what puts you at the table. Stay safe, young'un."

And with those last words, Mackmillions left the pod without everything he'd brought there with him. He left all to Bonez to distribute because everything he needed was out in the streets and would soon be at his fingertips.

"Pops!" Young Mack yelled out from the sunroof in the stretched Mercedes Benz truck. He dropped down after he spotted his pop and rushed out to greet him. "Damn, it's good to have you home already!" Young Mack held back the tears that threatened to expose his true love for his father.

"It's good to be home, son." Mackmillions laughed as he took his son in and rocked with him, not giving two fucks how sentimental they looked holding each other. "Now that's a face I haven't seen in a lifetime. How you holding, Max?" Mackmillions held back tears himself as he watched his long-time friend exit the vehicle followed by a grown-up version of a girl he once knew.

"Couldn't be much easier livin' outchea by myself," Max stated full of sarcasm.

"Yeah, I bet!" Mackmillions laughed hard then threw his left arm over Max's shoulder while keeping Young Mack under his right.

"Would you look at chu, Ms. Garcia." Mackmillions smiled at Aeriella.

She was looking stunning in a form-fitting Dior number with the crystal Dior strap heels. Her hair was mostly straight, but curled at the ends.

"Real beauty, right Pop?" Young Mack said, looking her over tastefully.

"Always has been," Mackmillions replied, giving her a slight head nod in approval.

"Thanks, Mr. Miller. You are quite a gentleman," Aeriella stated.

"Wh-what about me? Where's my props?"

"Whatever, Young Mack. You don't see me like you used to anymore," she shot down his efforts playfully.

"Fine as you are, I don't think God even sees you as he used to."

All three men laughed at that one before she playfully punched him in the stomach and turned, then climbed in the truck.

"You got some work to do," his father whispered in his ear.

"Tell me about it." Young Mack smiled in admiration and was determined to do just that.

Climbing inside the stretched vehicle felt like they'd entered a well-established nightclub. The vehicle was decked out with deep cushioned suede bench seats, a wet bar and sink, colored lights, a nice big plasma television, and the music blasted loud and clear through the Bose system.

"This is a bit much don't you think, son?"

"It's the only thing they had with a bulletproof exterior and Kevlar interior side panels for extra security. Plus they let my guy be our chauffeur free of charge." Young Mack tapped the divide and the window rolled down. "Pop, meet Josh, my head of security."

Mackmillions greeted the driver with a slight head nod and Josh did the same before he upped the window and drove past the green light at the intersection.

"So what's the order of business?" Young Mack couldn't think of the last time he'd smiled so much. He was truly glad that his father was back with him, plus he was feeling his liquor.

Mackmillions looked over to Max who grabbed one of his bags he'd brought with them from the trailer home.

"There's a lifetime of crime and evil in this bag. We have dirt on every single one of the greedy filthy bastards that thought it'd be nice to go against me."

"What are we gonna do with that?" Aeriella asked bringing all eyes to herself. "Whaaaat?" She was clearly embarrassed as the liquor did its thing with her too.

"We?" Young Mack shook his head at her.

"Okay, maybe I was just feeling the whole intensity of the situation," she said, then leaned back in her seat with a glass of liquor covering her face.

Young Mack smiled at her pouting face. He loved her loyalty and knew for sure she'd be down to get dirty, if need be.

"I've sat behind bars for fifteen years waiting for the day of judgement to come," Mackmillions stated as he looked inside at the contents in the bag.

"I'll 'andle tings myself dee boi got p'lice problemz," Max stated, speaking of Young Mack.

"That won't be a problem, I'm sure of that. It'll only be a matter of time before I have his charges dropped completely." Aeriella stood up for Young Mack.

"Bond or no bond, I ain't sitting shit out, Pops. You'll need all the help you can get. Surely you two can't be everywhere at once." Mackmillions' and Max's eyes met in amusement at Young Mack's last statement. "What's funny?"

"In our time, we've been told the exact opposite," Mackmillions confessed. "But never mind that. Can we get me outta these disaster relief clothes and into something more me!" Mackmillions lightened the mood.

"Almost forgot." Aeriella laughed before handing him a couple of bags from Nordstrom and Neiman Marcus.

After examining the designer threads, Mackmillions nodded in approval before accepting a bag from his son.

"What are these things?" he asked, looking at the black spiked Christian Louboutin red bottom sneakers.

"Those red bottoms, Pop, can't miss with 'em!" Young Mack laughed at the comical look his father gave his right-hand man, who just shrugged his shoulders at the high-end fashion.

"He's not lying, Mr. Miller. You'll fit in anywhere with those," Aeriella agreed.

"Okay, cool."

After calming himself, Young Mack knocked on the divide getting his drivers attention.

"'Sup bossman?" Josh asked once the window was lowered.

"Pull over and let her up front so Pop can change."

With a nod of his head, Josh did just as Young Mack requested. The look Aeriella gave Young Mack was one for the books and brought a chuckle even outta Max.

"What I say?" Young Mack asked once he noticed her facial expression.

"I'm surprised you two aren't married yet," Mackmillions spoke as he kicked off his shoes in preparation to change.

Aeriella climbed out and did as she knew to do. She really loved and respected Young Mack way more than she was willing to let him know. His situation with Ambrea was something she just didn't understand and she wasn't ready to let him have a chance to break her heart. It's why she gave him such a hard time all the time.

"She's a good woman," Young Mack stated, trying to suppress his true feelings.

"She really is, son, and you better tighten your game up if you want her in your corner. She's a well-established queen, and only a real king will be able to capture her heart."

"That's deep, Pop. How you read all that about her?"

"Reminds me of the one and only true queen that captured mine and vice versa. Anywho, Max, our first order of business is finding a place for me to lay my head," Mackmillions stated while getting dressed. Young Mack smiled at all the bundled-up money Max exposed in one of the other bags. "That's how you coming?"

"Rainy day stash." Mackmillions smiled.

"Well, you better keep it because we still have our home."

"Home home?" Mackmillions asked with wide-eyed surprise.

"Home was in Ma's name and I've been keeping a cleaning crew on call there every six months in case Ma ever shook back and wanted to be home," Young Mack explained.

"Damn, son, that's that good ole fashioned me coming outta you."

They all laughed at his comical tone before going over all that they needed to discuss.

"Now that we're past that, let's have fun tonight, but after tonight, it's all work, no sleep," Mackmillions ordered.

"That's a bill, Pop!"

Max nodded his head and kept his eyes fixed outside of the vehicle. The music in the stretch suddenly stopped and Josh lowered the window between them. "We have a tail, boys."

"It's to be expected, Max. They know I'm here."

"And so do we know of them."

His blood red eyes seemed to never turn white and it gave him a definite look of death.

"What's the order, bossman?" Josh asked, looking to Young Mack through the rearview mirror.

"It's cool," both Young Mack and his father stated in unison.

"Oookkkaaayyy, now that was weird." Aeriella laughed.

"No sweat, Josh. Just do you like they don't exist, but you climb yo' sexy ass back here and give the kid some attention."

She wasn't sure what made her do it, but she did just as he requested and climbed through the dividing window before Josh let it back up.

"That's my girl." Young Mack laughed as she walked over and sat in his lap.

"Guess we gotta move quicker than we thought." Mackmillions looked to Max.

"Guess so," was Max's only reply.

Chapter 4

"Yo! Fuck outta here with all that smacking shit, my dude!" Agent Chandler couldn't believe how much of a pig his partner was around the clock.

"Yo! You's buggin', bee," Agent Drexler mocked his New York partner's accent with a mouth full of Krispy Kreme donut.

The two were assigned to Mackentosh Miller's confidential detail. Chandler shook his head at his overweight partner. He could be disgusting at times, like now, as he made animalistic noises while chowing down a full dozen of cinnamon-powdered donuts. He himself was what he'd often been called around the Bureau, but never admitted to, a body freak. He loved his physique and praised his workouts. Women admired him everywhere he went, and he loved the attention being sexy got him. Even more, he loved the fun he often had with the women of all shades in life.

"You's a whole pig on the real, Drex," Chandler stated before turning his attention back to the massive home their subject had been holed up in for hours.

"I may be a pig, true, but bruh, you a whole male thot with all your tight-ass clothes your muscles be stretching out of, not to mention them pretty boy haircuts."

"Fuck outta here," Chandler said just as his phone rang, interrupting them.

"Nawl, seriously though, do you think I could join the male thot club? I mean, I could get fine like you think you are too."

"Saved by the bell," he stated before answering his phone.

"What's going on out there?" spoke Senior Agent Gamble, questioning the status of the operation he had personally ordered.

"Not much of nothing, same as a few hours ago when you called."

"You getting sweet with me, New York?" Gamble caught the underlying irritation evident in the agent's tone.

"Just ready for a job that comes with some action. Seems like we keep getting these tag-along gigs." Chandler stated his truth and kept it a gee with him.

"Just keep your damn eyes peeled open and your smart-ass mouth wired shut, Agent," Gamble shot back as he thought of the irony in what Chandler said and the vital caution he "forgot" to warn them to utilize.

"Yeah, yeah, we got it."

"Oh, and New York?"

"Yeah?"

"Be careful what you ask for." Gamble chuckled before ending their call.

"Don't sweat what he says, man. He's always been a bit of an asshole," Drexler said after watching his partner's mood change. He'd heard the short dialogue between them and knew his partner was feeling some type of way.

"Be careful what I ask for? His old ass must not know my get down," Chandler was heated and needed a release for the boredom.

"I don't know, Cee, it's like something off about this detail when I think about it. He has us following behind a dude that's been in the pen since you and I were in grade school or some shit like that. What could this guy really have going on that warrants two very skilled agents to be following him after his very first minute outta prison? Shit just don't make any sense to me. But what do I know besides that food was God's real blessing to his children."

"See, you can be a real dick sometimes."

"What I say?" Drexler asked comically.

"Just when you are beginning to make a little sense for a change, you go and snatch that shit right outta my mind with your sinful-ass gluttony."

"Damn, that's heavy, Cee."

"Just calling a quarter a quarter, Drex," Chandler stated with no remorse.

"Nawl, I only said that because I'm over here getting hungry while eating all these snacks and shit." Drexler laughed, and crumbs flew from his chubby cheeks and out of his mouth, crash landing on the dashboard.

Pig! Chandler thought to himself but couldn't be certain his laughter from his foolish partner.

$$$$$

"They still out there, Pop," Young Mack stated as he watched the unmarked vehicle sitting fifty yards out.

"Yeah, I figured that. Max, this tail is personal and they need to be shaken up a bit. Go out there and let them know we know they're there and maybe, just maybe, that'll get 'em off us for a few days tops."

Mackmillions knew his adversaries wouldn't completely reveal their hands to him and they definitely weren't about to allow him to roam the city unwatched. He was too much of a threat to their careers and more importantly, he was too much of a threat to their lives.

"I'll have my team pull up and assist you. Josh, call the boys and tell them to get here pronto from the opposite end of the block so they can box the car off from fleeing us."

Young Mack gave the order and it was done immediately.

"Son," Mackmillions called out to Young Mack before he left his presence.

"What up, Pop?"

"Your mother?"

"Say less. I'm on it."

Young Mack smiled on the inside as he climbed the stairs in their family home. He thought about everything that was going on around him, and the fact that his father was thinking about his mother only meant one thing. He chuckled to himself before stepping through the door of his old bedroom, where Aeriella sat heavily engrossed in her laptop.

"Am I interrupting?" he asked as he closed the door behind him.

"Nah, just having fun talking to my girls back in Georgia on live chat." She smiled big.

"Live chat, huh?" Young Mack said before kicking his shoes off and joining her on the bed, being sure to slide behind her juiciness.

"Uhhh, excuse me, Ms. Lady, who is that and is he yours?" one of her girlfriends spoke up once he could be seen by them all.

"Ladies, be good now, this is Mackentosh Miller the second."

"Damn, he is handsome, gurrrl!"

"My point exactly," agreed the first one to speak.

"Mack, this is Debra at the top right."

"Hi Mack," Debra spoke.

"Chantel is top left."

"Hey sexy," Chantel flirted, as she was the first one to acknowledge him on screen.

"Okaaay, this is Rahmilla, bottom right, and Jackie is at her left."

The last two women smiled and waved politely.

"Hi ladies, it's nice to meet y'all."

"Ditto!" all the ladies said in unison. "Guess I'll let you get back to it then." Young Mack smiled and nodded his head at the computer screen before whispering a little something in her ear and kissing her cheek with a chuckle. "Hope I didn't embarrass you," he said, then jumped outta bed to leave.

"Where are you going?" she asked after lowering her laptop screen.

"Nowhere, ma, you clocking or what?"

"Or what," Aeriella replied with her lips twisted.

"We both know the real though, so you can keep fronting like that all you want to. Anyways, I'm 'bout to slide out here and make sure my men do exactly what's needed to get these people off Pops' back."

"Be careful," she stated genuinely.

"Always, ma. Now get back to chatting with my new fan base and tell 'em I'm team follow back on IG." He laughed before leaving his room and closing the door behind him.

$$$$$

"This shit is really dead out here," Agent Drexler said as he tossed the empty box from the dozen donuts he'd consumed without the help of his partner.

"Yeah, shit's dead for real," Chandler agreed with his partner.

"What say we dip off and hit up Frenchie's for some of that famous southern fried chicken?" Drexler could already taste the succulent seasoning mixed with grease as if it were hot on his tongue.

"Dude, you just maxed out a whole dozen donuts. You can't be serious."

"As an old person tryna avoid the Corona. My appetite ain't nothing to play with, my boy. I feel like if I'm not eating, then my entire body would shut off and I'll die from starvation."

"Kid, you're just gluttonous," Chandler stated seriously.

"Nawl, that's a sin. I just eat to be comfortable, not to get full," Drexler stated as if his words were the gospel.

"You're sad, Drex!" Chandler said as he watched a pair of headlights coming up from their rearview mirror.

"Yeah, I'm sad because I need to eat some real food."

"Hands up, bitch boys and keep 'em there!" A masked man appeared out of the night's thin air.

Chandler never got a chance to turn around after hearing the demands of the masked man before cold steel was being pressed into the back of his head through the lowered window.

"Alright, you guys, just calm down," Agent Chandler stated as if the situation was in his hands.

"Calm down? Bitch, this is us being calm. Or would you like to see what us being rowdy feels like?"

"Stop talking," a voice came from behind the agents, and all noise ceased. "Fuck ya doin' round 'ere noopin' and carryin' on fa'?" Max asked, standing next to one of Young Mack's soldiers.

"Shit ain't what it seems," Chandler started, but he was cut off by his brainless partner.

"Man, we're federal agents, dawg, and if y'all kill us, the Bureau will hunt you mu'fuckas down!" Agent Drexler said in a heated panic as sweat began to drench his face.

"Why would federal agents sit outside a home where nobody lives?" Young Mack's voice came from behind Drexler. There was no way he was missing out on something like this.

"It's just our assignment, bruh. We don't get to choose where we work," Chandler spoke in their defense.

"Well spoken, Agent…?"

"Chandler, and I'm Agent Drexler. We the best of the best, so if y'all kill us, we huntin' y'all asses, straight up!"

"If we kill y'all, how will you hunt us?" one of Young Mack's men asked, humored by the fat one.

"Fuck all that! We don't need to see no badges because we'll take y'all's word on it, plus we thought this was something of a different stroke." Young Mack chuckled.

"But, ummm, you guys be safe and, umm, tell your bosses we know they're here, and thanks for the heads up."

"What the fuck?" Drexler exhaled as the car in front of them revved its engine with its reverse lights glowing. "Let's get the hell outta here, Cee, these mu'fuckas are on to us!"

"No shit! You don't think I see this fuckery?" Chandler was heated, and the only thing he could think of were Gamble's last words in the last phone call.

Agent Chandler drove in deep thought about what had just transpired. Never in all of his career had he accepted a mu'fucka putting a weapon to his head and make it away to talk about it. He'd never not had the ups on the criminals he was investigating, but Senior Agent Gamble had just put his life on the line, and he definitely needed to find out why.

$$\$\$\$\$\$$

Senior Agent Gamble was in the middle of a meeting when Chandler stormed in unannounced. The look the two gave one another matched in anger, and even though Gamble was his superior, Chandler wasn't calming down until he got answers.

"Let's break for half an hour. My apologies. And as you can see, the kids need their attention too."

Agent Chandler didn't pay any of the salty looks any attention as other agents, some above and others below him, passed. Gamble could clearly see the steam coming from the young and certainly thriving agent now sitting at the far end of the conference table.

"I see you must've gotten what you wished for?" Gamble chuckled.

"My life is not a fucking play token, and I don't take kindly to being in the fucking dark when I'm out in the field!" Chandler stated, folding his thick arms across his chest for emphasis.

"First, watch your mouth, you little piece of shit paper. Second, you are an agent of this Bureau, and when an assignment is handed down, you do your fucking duty to this country with no fucking questions asked. I'm pretty sure you haven't accomplished all that you have by being a little pissy-mouthed baby when shit hits you in the face."

Gamble truly didn't approve of Agent Chandler's transfer down to Houston like most of the higher ups did. Truth is, he knew the smart-mouthed agent would only get in his way of doing things the way he was so used to doing them. He'd read and observed all the reports on the agent back in New York and couldn't shake the feeling that he was being placed within his ranks to disrupt his order. He knew the agent was also a hot-headed do-gooder, but the fact that he got the job done at a rate higher then he'd ever witnessed firsthand was enough for his colleagues to summon the advancing agent.

"You prejudiced son of a bitch! You sent me and my partner on this close tail detail and you somehow forget to tell us how dangerous these muthafuckers are," Chandler stated, slamming his fist into the table.

"You sound like a fucking rookie pussy. You've been crying about this and crying about that since you pulled up, and now you get a little surprise action out in the field and you come running to Papa like a little spoiled brat. Drexler called and told me about the little run-in. Well, learn the rules out here before you go parking a damn stakeout detail on the perp's PRIVATE PROPERTY!" Gamble yelled.

"I'm a fucking federal agent. There is no such thing as private property! Mu'fucka come waving weapons and shit and we're supposed to just let that shit ride with no retaliation?"

"Did you see any weapons? Did you even see any faces or any signs of identification to which we could charge someone with a crime, Chander?" Gamble wasn't up on every detail of the situation, but he knew Mackmillions and his organization, though deflated, were anything but amateurs.

Chandler's silence answered his questions and made him angrier.

"This is the south, and you better get familiar with how it goes here. Focus on doing your job, Agent. Nothing more and nothing less."

"So I'm to forget this even happened?" Chandler asked, needing to hear the answer come from his mouth.

"Tell me who to go after and I'll have warrants for every known place in every county in this city. Who did you I.D.?"

A moment of silence passed between them. Gamble knew the agent was mad, but there really wasn't anything they could do without him or his partner identifying anyone. Not that he would if they could. His intentions were much worse than another prison cell for Mackentosh Mackmillions Miller.

"Thanks for nothing!" Chandler exclaimed after having his hand full of the jerk before him. He wasn't sure how to handle things, but one thing was for certain, and that was that he wasn't about to just sit on his hands. He shook his head in disgust at the senior agent before standing from his seat and leaving the conference room slamming the door behind him.

Gamble quickly whipped out his personal phone and turned around in his chair to call a very close friend and business associate.

"Talk to me," the voice on the other end of the phone said.

"Chandler is heated after our guy got away with the stunt they pulled on him and his partner," Gamble stated firmly.

"I'm sorry I missed the point."

"We need to get our shit together before this knucklehead fucks around and finds out, that's the point." Gamble couldn't believe the audacity of this one.

"Calm down. Everything is in order, and as long as you light Chandler's asshole on fire with our guy, he'll do everything for us and we won't even have to lift a finger."

Gamble knew he was right, and it was a part of why they wanted the hot-headed agent there in the first place.

"I'll douse his ass with diesel if that's what it'll take. But let's make sure our problem gets taken care of before we have other kind of problems like the one brewing with this one."

"You do that and we'll stay on top. By the way, have you checked your mailbox today? I heard stimulus checks came around again tenfold."

Gamble smiled at the revelation as the other end of the call went dead.

More money meant more liquor and definitely more pussy. He'd grown obsessed with the

taste, natural smell, and feel of black pussy and knew just the spot to get his rocks off the right way.

$$\$\$\$\$\$$

"So what is it?"

"All property and business owned by your pop is part of the Realm's order for its members,

but the good thing is, now it all belongs to you," KenKen stated after reviewing Rob's signatures and securing the contracts.

"You keep speaking of this Realm, but if my father wouldn't cooperate with their rules, what makes you so confident that I will, especially after acquiring all this?" Rob emphasized with his arms spread wide.

"All of what?" KenKen asked while looking around the office where they were with a disapproved expression. "Listen, Rob, I know this is all new to you, but these things you just signed your name on only makes you a legitimate businessman and a millionaire to society. It's a demand from the head members of the Realm that each chairman meets the financial standing of accomplished millionaires in order to divert unwanted government attention. So, don't think for a minute that I'm convinced that you'll make it in this thing, but what I'm confident in is the matter of you still being as broke now as you were before you signed the documents." KenKen relaxed in his seat and allowed his words to resonate.

"How does all this work, and why am I now a part of it?"

"You're a part of it because like everyone with sense, you wanna live. We'll figure out how you can work it as you grow to understand the ways of this world."

"Fuck made you overseer of me?" Rob wanted to know.

"Same mu'fuckas who made me overseer of your father. Hell, and if I outlive you, I'll be overseer to your bloodline as well. Look, Rob, taking this position has its down sides, but the best thing about it is that it removes your mother completely outta harm's way, as she will be protected and not held responsible for anything your father had undertook with the Realm. It gets passed down to your wife, but being that you're not married and have no kids, heavy is the crown of the king."

"King? Shit, I feel like a flunky," Rob confessed.

"So, what's the upside to being a flunky?" KenKen asked before checking the time on his watch.

"Hell, a flunky is a flunky, bottom of the barrel."

"That's the downside of it. Always find the upside in all things if you wanna survive this lifestyle, Rob."

"Well, you tell me what's the upside in all this, smart guy?"

"Everyone looks over a flunky and that makes them underestimated while they have nothing to lose, but everything to gain," KenKen jeweled him. "Let's go. I have some important people you need to meet."

Rob's eyes lowered as they adjusted to the darkened club atmosphere. He remembered the very first time walking into this very place the night he met the man who was, unbeknownst to him, his father. He'd nearly lost his life in the same confines of the office they'd just walked out of.

Being the new owner of Club Ambitions would be a real life-changer for him.

As they made their way through the crowded establishment on the way to the VIP section, Rob caught the eyes of a sexy-ass bartender covered in tattoos watching their every move.

"What's the business, big Ken?" one of the bouncers at the rope of the VIP section asked after noticing them step that way.

"Same ole same ole, Pop, how you holding?" KenKen responded with a thug pound on the bouncer's massive hand.

"I'm just living, my guy, you know me. Who this you got wit' you tonight?" The guy eyed Rob and immediately remembered him.

"Hell, I'm with him. The man owns the place now." KenKen smiled at the man's shocked expression. He also saw the earlier looks Pop was throwing at Rob as he was trying to little man him.

"How 'bout that," Pop stated, clearly shocked.

"Why are we still standing here?" Rob asked KenKen while ignoring the bouncer's extended hand.

"Don't ask me. Ask your worker." KenKen laughed.

"Rope," Rob demanded, and Pop complied immediately.

"In exactly two hours, gather all your coworkers and meet me at that bar over there, and make sure it's cleared for me to get there," Rob ordered, and Pop nodded his understanding.

He purposely chose the bar with the tattooed hottie in order to make an impression with her. After locking eyes with her again to let her know he knew she was watching, he turned and made his way into the VIP section, where KenKen sat comfortably engrossed in conversation with two heavyset white men in suits.

"Let me guess: Rob, am I right?" One of the suits stood and shook his hand.

"Yeah, and you are?"

"Call me the Lamb, and this here is my cohort, the Goat," the man spoke before touching drink glasses with his partner.

"Members of the Realm?"

"You guessed it, Junior. Now how about you be careful using that pseudonym? We don't exist," the other suit said and stood to hand Rob a drink. He accepted. "Now that introductions are done, let's have a drink and get down to business."

To that, everyone raised their drinks and drank the stiff shots of Henn.

"These guys are the reason your father never saw the insides of a prison cell," KenKen opened the floor.

"It's why all names and associations must remain anonymous in every way possible," The Goat spoke up before taking another shot of the dark liquor.

The duo had the perfect names. One seemed too sheepish to even be involved with something like they were, but Rob knew that looks could always be deceiving. The other seemed aggressive and hot to the head, something typical from a pig of his caliber. The Lamb and the Goat.

"Yes, for all of our safety." The Lamb nodded politely.

"I get it. Now what's up with this business you mentioned?"

"Just like his dad, so eager to get down to business. Well, for us to secure your safety from prosecution, it's gonna cost you a third of the revenue brought in on the heroin and half of what comes in from the coke."

Rob looked to KenKen for guidance on the matter because they hadn't talked about any dope nor coke transactions.

"From the look on your face, I'm assuming the price will be a problem?" the Lamb asked in a very unfriendly manner, unusual from what he'd displayed so far.

"Always is, partner," the Goat added his two cents.

"If it were a problem, I would say so with my mouth and not with my looks. I haven't been informed of any affairs of my father's as of yet to make assessments on anything of that nature right now," Rob explained honestly.

"You need time?" the Lamb assessed the situation for what it was.

"Yes."

"Twenty-four hours," the Goat jumped in.

"Cool, but the next time we meet in my establishment, there will be no liquor for you before business, because I'm itching to knock yo' fucking face off already," Rob growled at the overweight white man.

"Fu——"

"Hey!" The Lamb stood up between them. "Kill that shit, will you!"

KenKen never moved an inch, but the glizzy on his thigh was worth a million words.

"Yeah, you're right. Me and this brown don't mix."

Rob caught the racial remark even though he set down the Hennessey bottle he'd grabbed as if he was gonna hit him with it.

"Nobody alive can intimidate me, so you can cut the tough guy act, because it won't work on me. I'm with the dumb shit all day long. Hell, I tried to kill my father. It's how we met, and I've put one through my own mother, so pain don't register either. Don't try to apply pressure where it isn't warranted, agent, because pressure doesn't only burst pipes. It activates switches. Whatever our dealings are, they will be done with precision."

"Just make sure of that, and we'll be straight," the Lamb said with an outreached hand.

Rob shook it, but made no effort to do the same with the other guy.

"Come on, let's hit that strip joint you enjoy so much." The Lamb collected his partner and they left without incident.

"I don't like him." Rob expressed what anyone with eyes could see.

"Of course you don't. He's a Fed. But you need to learn how to coexist with him if you wanna remain free in these streets, young homie."

"I can dig it." Rob nodded his head before looking to the bar, where a small crowd had formed.

"Good. Now go handle your business with your new crew. They're a solid bunch," KenKen stated before signaling to a bottle girl with a fat ass and some deep dimples.

Rob made his way over to the bar and introduced himself to the staff as their new boss, and everyone greeted him accordingly. Things went smooth with the restructuring, and everyone took their new titles to heart and were eager to prove themselves worthy of them. One in particular.

"What's your name?" Rob asked as she couldn't tear her eyes away from his.

"Gianna, but everyone calls me Gigi."

Rob couldn't take his eyes off of her either, and he loved the fact that he didn't intimidate her even after he revealed his new status.

"Alright, that's it. Y'all can get to your jobs now!" He dismissed the rest of them, but held her attention. She knew better to leave and miss out on opportunity to secure her position with her new boss.

"I guess I'll be needed for reasons that your mouth hasn't said, but your eyes are," Gigi spoke seductively. The look in her eyes said she'd be down for whatever.

"Long night tonight, ma. Maybe we can check it some other time," Rob lied.

"I ain't got shit to do tonight, so I could wait up if you'd like me to."

After watching her juicy tongue glide across those sexy lips, he was done for.

"Yeah, that'll be perfect." He smiled, then slid her his phone before turning to leave.

"You forgetting something!" she yelled over the loud music.

"I'll hit you when I'm ready for you!" he replied with a wink.

"Glad to know." Gigi smiled to herself as he disappeared in the crowded club, leaving her panties soaked.

Chapter 5

"Ambrea!"

"Yes, my love, I'm here." Ambrea loved being submissive to her new husband.

Everything in their life together had been great, even from the beginning. Well, she did have one problem, and if she had to choose, she'd die without telling a soul about it.

"Geez, you are beautiful, mami. It's like I see you for the first time every time I lay eyes on you." Gurdo smiled and kissed her lips gracefully.

"Thank you, baby, and you don't look too bad yourself," she playfully stated before kissing his lips.

"Look too bad? Honey, I've dropped fifty pounds since we've been here. Can I at least get an A for effort," he spoke playfully with pouted lips.

"Aww, mami's baby, mwah! Sure can, baby, because you look good enough to eat." She laughed at his theatrics.

"Mmm, that's what I'm talking about." Gurdo laughed as he lifted her up in the air, displaying his new strength.

Ambrea wrapped her legs around her man's waist and stared in his eyes. He was everything she ever wanted in a man. Wealthy beyond all means, loving and very attentive to all her needs, and she had always found him attractive, even before the major weight transformation. But like all good things in life, there was one flaw to her king, and it was a dreaded one. He was unsuccessful in fulfilling her sexual desires, and it was the one thing that kept her close to her ultimate secret.

"You know there is business I have to handle before we leave and go back to the States," he calmly admitted. One thing he hated more than anything was making her feel as if anything came before her.

"Of course I know, baby, and I respect you for always thinking of me the way you do."

"Gotta make sure my wifey right, know what I mean?" He smiled.

"I love you." Ambrea kissed his lips while holding his face in her hands.

"I know you do. It's why I love you so much."

"Why, because I love you?"

"No, because you're not afraid to love me with or without my position."

Gurdo was the successor of his father's very successful drug empire and had amassed nearly two hundred million dollars since his reign began only four years prior. He did business all over the United States and in some small countries and was now looking to broaden the scope of his empire's product line.

After spending all night satisfying her husband, Ambrea woke up to an empty bed and a burning desire to be pleased herself.

"What have I done?" she questioned herself, hating now sexually frustrated she was. She had heard it all her life whether from her mother or her aunties and most times even from her girls that it would be suicide for a woman to marry a man that couldn't satisfy her in bed.

Back when marriage was the furthest thought from her mind, those words meant absolutely nothing, and now she woke with a pressure she wished her husband could release. Those words she heard so often growing up were eating at her, and it felt like all the bites were centered directly against her kitty. She didn't regret getting married to Gurdo because she knew without a shadow of a doubt that she loved him, but she hated her own decision to be so stingy with the kat growing up. Maybe she'd have experienced enough orgasms to last her a lifetime and it would make her relationship and marriage perfect. Unbeknownst to Young Mack and the rest of the world, he was her first, and besides her boyfriend and now husband, Gurdo, no other man dead or alive had ever made it all the way with her sexually.

Frustrated, she threw the cover and sheets from her body and climbed out of bed, still in the nude. She loved sleeping that way. It was something Young Mack introduced her to, and it stuck with her. Instantly, she looked to the night stand next to the bed and picked up her phone and made her way inside of the master bedroom to take a shower and relieve herself. After stepping inside of the floor to ceiling glass doors to the shower, she adjusted the water until it was hot enough to burn her skin a little. Being away from their Houston home killed the chance of implementing her toys for a quick session, but she had back up hidden within her cell phone. She hurriedly uploaded the footage she had there of her and Young Mack's many heated sessions, then selected her favorite one. She'd been secretly recording them for a while before she finally came out and told him. The news amplified his passion and she loved it. Thinking back on the actual encounters, she smiled at how much he accused her of being addicted to him. Boy, he really did not know how on point he was back then and even until now, or maybe he did and that's why he sexed her so damn good, so often. She didn't hate herself for cheating on Gurdo. Hell, she needed as much satisfaction as she provided for him sexually, and Young Mack was that and more.

The video she uploaded was the very first time he introduced her to anal sex. She fast forwarded the clip of their heavy foreplay session and got straight into the action. She watched hungrily as he pounded her from the back as she laid with her chest on the bed and her ass and pussy sitting perfect for his deep strokes. The action in the video was having its intended effects on her because her juices were flowing thickly down her leg as she manipulated her pulsating clitoris. Moans escaped her mouth as she temporarily shut her eyes due to the sensations coursing through her body. The sexually satisfying sounds coming from her phone forced her eyes to reopen and witness Young Mack turning her so that she was positioned on her back. Lifting her knees until they were flush against her sensitive breasts, he made her hold them there while he stroked her hard and fast, pleasing them both to no ends. Her first climax ripped through her like a storm as she watched herself being dominated by his powerful performance. Her essence filled her hand as the action picked up in the video. Young Mack swiftly pulled out of her wetness and smoothly entered her tight nether hole. She remembered the tight pressure in that moment and squeezed her thighs together, capturing her hand, but it didn't stop her fingers from doing their job inside of her. Sweat glistened on Young Mack's athletic figure, highlighting his powerful strokes in and out of her body. The euphoric boil deep in her core rushed through her, causing her back to arch and her knees began to buckle. Seeing herself being conquered mixed with her expert administrations quickly became too much for her. An orgasm tore through her and she fell to the shower floor flat on her ass. Her legs shook uncontrollably, and tears filled her eyelids as she fought to catch her breath while watching her fluids spray freely from her sex.

The pleasure of the explosive orgasm lasted five whole minutes - the length remaining on the sex scene. She slowly lifted herself from the floor, holding a tight grip on the towel rack. Her clit tingled once her thighs came together and caused her to cuff her sex with her palm centered on her sensitive button.

"Damn!" she exhaled while looking down over her phone. "Dick'll make a bitch jump from the tallest building ever created." She laughed at her humorous thoughts while picking her phone up and placing it in the soap holder.

Stepping underneath the steady stream of the hot water was so relaxing and soothing to her fulfilled body. She lathered the loofah with her favorite Vera Wang body wash and thoroughly scrubbed herself before the sound of the bathroom door caught her attention.

"Hola?" a soft feminine voice spoke from the door.

"Yes, may I help you?" Ambrea asked while wrapping herself in a huge towel and stepping from the shower.

"Me so sorry, come different time!" the very pretty Spanish girl stated in a rushed panic.

"No, no, no, it's okay. Are you here to clean?" Ambrea stopped her by grabbing her arm tightly.

"Sí, senorita," the young lady replied.

"Come do your job. I am finished here." Ambrea released her arm and moved past her so she couldn't argue. She quickly found the king-sized bed that screamed out to her.

Sleep must've found her without her permission because she was having the best dream and the sensations were undeniable - that was, until she felt real pressure on her sex with the slight invasion of teeth. Her eyes staggered open and the sight of her husband staring back at her eased her tension.

"Thank you for taking care of me last night, my love," he said before wrapping his lips back around her hardened nub.

Gurdo was convinced that his new wife was the one for him. He'd never gone down on any woman before her and was learning to love the act. Flicking his tongue in ways he'd never done before, he knew she was enjoying him by the way her body rocked and humped against his mouth.

"Ssss, baby, you're making me feel so good right now!" Ambrea moaned in pleasure.

"Cum for me, love, I need to taste you," he said between applying pressure on her pussy with his tongue flattened.

His skills were average at best, and she hated that it was so challenging for her to climax from his efforts. Her mind instinctively went back to the video she'd watched earlier in the shower in order to bring herself to orgasm and like magic, her juices rushed through her and soaked his face. He reveled in her sweet nectar and strengthened his efforts by adding first one then two and finally three fingers inside of her slickened treasure. The pleasure took her over the edge again and he watched as she released herself. A sinister smile crept onto his face after he worshipped her inner thighs and all over her goodies.

"I absolutely love how you taste," he confessed while rising to his feet.

"I really needed that," she lied to boost his ego.

No man alive nor dead would honestly be okay with not being able to please his woman, especially not one as beautiful as her.

"It's been a long day and I need to shower and catch up on some sleep before we jet outta here in the morning," Gurdo said, then smoothly made his way into the bathroom.

"Oh shit!" She remembered leaving her phone in the shower. Goosebumps spread all over her body as the possibility of being discovered radiated in her mind.

Just as extreme panic began to set in, she looked to the night stand and noticed her phone lying face down on top of it. That was odd, because she clearly remembered leaving it in the soap holder. She released a deep sigh before picking up her phone, only to see a note stuck to its screen. After reading the note, she quickly balled it up and her heart began beating against her chest like a drummer hitting his drums.

"Fuck!"

$$$$$

"Whaaat?" Young Mack sat up in bed shocked by Ambrea's revelation.

"I don't know what to do," she sniffed as he listened closely.

"What did the note say exactly?" he asked fully awake now.

"The bitch just said she has copies of my secrets and wonders what my rich husband would think of them," Ambrea cried.

"Calm down, ma, she probably just wants money. Did she leave a number?"

"Yeah, she programmed it as my wallpaper."

"Damn."

"What am I to do?" Ambrea was tearing herself apart.

"Are you at the villa now?" he asked hopefully.

"Yeah, but I've looked everywhere and she's nowhere to be found. None of these people clearly understand English enough to talk to me."

"That's heavy."

"Yeah, and we're leaving in a few hours."

"Don't panic. Just get to me as fast as possible and we'll make the call together, okay?"

"We have to take care of this issue or our lives will be ruined, if not lost." Ambrea was thinking of the worst.

"I feel you, ma, but stop thinking like that. We'll handle it," Young Mack assured her.

"I love you Mack," she stated wholeheartedly.

"You better, and next time you decide to turn ghost for months, you won't have to worry about some leaked videos. I'll be your biggest problem."

"Yes, daddy, I got you."

"Now tell me you love me again and go ahead and get you some rest, love."

"I love you," Ambrea swore before ending their call.

Fuck! Young Mack thought as he hopped outta bed.

He thought hard as possible about how they could crawl their way out of this one. Going into his closet, he thought about how valuable the dollar was in Mexico. His safe was nice and he could spare to release a few grand to make this issue go away.

"Easy peasy," he said to himself and removed five neatly-wrapped stacks of blue hundreds from his safe.

The thought of brining more occurred, but with the value of the US dollar being ten times it's worth he figured fifty thousand would make a mu'fucka sell their own mother.

He secured the money in a Gucci fanny pack before getting himself dressed

for the day. His father had him set out to accomplish something, and tonight was the night he planned to make it all come together. He stepped into his bathroom and nearly jumped out of his skin when he saw Aeriella sitting on the toilet typing away on her personal laptop.

"Shit!" he gasped, but was glad that she had her ear buds in her ears.

"Hey you," she looked up with a bright smile on her angelic face.

"Hey you too." Young Mack returned her smile and leaned up against the open door frame.

"Sorry for scaring you," she chuckled before looking back at her laptop screen.

"Scaring who? Woman, please, I'm Gucci, love." Young Mack playfully blew her off.

"Well, my service down the hall was giving me trouble so I hope you don't mind me breaking in here like this. I'm kinda working on your case."

"You good, ma. But what if I decided to come in here naked? And with a stiffy, on my way to piss, or better yet whack the——"

"Whoooa, TMI! Do I need to make an exit?" Aeriella blushed from him being so open with her. She loved it, but couldn't tell him that - at least not yet.

"I mean, by now it would be too late to think about that, so what would you do if I did come through like that, scaredy cat?"

"First of all, I'm grown and I know how to handle mines when the occasion arises. But don't be getting your hopes up too high now that I'm living here with you."

"Woman, ain't nobody worried about you like that," he lied.

Aeriella stood to her feet with her laptop out in front of her. Young Mack was having an effect on her like always, but she was determined to make him work for it.

"Well, baby Mack seems to see things differently," Aeriella looked down on the clearly visible bulge in his designer jeans and his eyes followed.

"You've always been able to tell when I'm lying," he laughed.

"Yep!" she smiled seductively before brushing past him.

The view of her tight booty shorts wedged between her womanly lips was doing something to him. When she stood up, there was no way for him to hide his arousal, plus the view of those shorts cutting between her juicy cheeks was too much.

"Come here real quick, ma," he stated while grabbing her around her small waist.

"What is it, Mackentosh?" She feigned irritation.

"Why you do me this way? It's been months and you haven't as much as let me hold you at night."

"That's because we both know what would happen if I did," she replied while turning to face him.

"And what's so wrong with that?" he asked as he stared deep into her eyes.

"First, you are a man whore," she laughed.

"No I'm not, what the fuck?" He laughed with her.

"Okay, I'm joking, but there are things we have to figure out about each other that we don't know about before we can cross that line."

"I hear you."

"I know you do, but understand one thing. If I put you in this pussy…" She placed his hand between her legs to feel her heat. "You and I will never be apart again, which means we'll have to take each other as we are, and that's what I'm afraid of." She stood on her tiptoes and kissed his lips for the first time since they'd been reunited.

"Say that shit then." He smiled as she made her exit, stopping in the door of his bedroom to look back at him before disappearing.

After doing his hygiene, Young Mack grabbed his bag filled with money and informed his security team that he was stepping out, but needed them to stay with Aeriella. Of course Josh wasn't feeling that and gave protest, but Young Mack informed him that he wouldn't be alone and would be back soon.

Young Mack jumped inside his brand-new Cadillac Escalade 500 and called his guy to inform him that he was on his way over. Twenty minutes later, he pulled up to the exclusive neighborhood out in Lake Olympia that his guys decided would be a good place for their operation outside of the ghetto.

"Blaaat! Blaaat! What's poppin', gangsta?" K-Dawg yelled. His massive stature was covered in tattoos and like always, he wasn't wearing a shirt to conceal his upper body.

"What's hittin', kid? And why yo' ass ain't never got a shirt on?" Young Mack shook up with his homie and shared a hug.

"Because I'm me, and no other reason matters." K-Dawg laughed loudly.

"Look, I know the fellas would love to kick the shit, but I got a move to make and I need you with me."

"Heavy duty or lightweight?" K-Dawg immediately got serious once he heard that.

"Lightweight, of course," Young Mack replied.

"Light heavy it is, then," K-Dawg said and rushed into the huge home before Young Mack could protest.

Young Mack shook his head as he watched his men pour out of the house, weapons in hand and ready for whatever.

"What's happenin'?" Deuce asked followed by Hogg, Pooh, and Rolla.

"Salute, my gangstas," Young Mack stated before showing his man some love.

"K-Dawg said trouble was out here," Pooh said, releasing his big homie from their gangsta embrace.

"Nawl, probably just wanted y'all to see me before we slide out."

"Slide out to where? I know we rollin' too." Deuce stepped up.

"Nawl, we just about to grab the queen and deliver her to her king, nah'mean?"

"For shit sho'. Shiiit, as long as Pops been away, that's way overdue," Deuce said, dapping him up once again as K-Dawg appeared with a duffle bag in his right hand.

"Alright, Mike Lawry." Deuce jabbed at how well-dressed his homie was.

"That nigga love his suits. I love not wearing mine." K-Dawg laughed and dapped his team up before getting behind the wheel of Young Mack's truck. "So where to?"

"It's programmed in the GPS," Young Mack replied without looking up from texting on his phone.

"Say less," K-Dawg replied, then turned up the sound of YFN spitting his hood classic "7.62".

$$$$$

"Bossman, we need to gas up real quick. You need something outta here?" Pop asked as he pulled into the Shell gas station.

"I got all I need right here, my dude," Rob stated while roughly gripping Gianna's thigh.

"Cool. Monsta, stay on point," Pop ordered his little brother, who was riding shotgun in Rob's brand new Mercedes Maybach.

"What do you have planned for tonight, love?" Gigi asked while rolling up a fatty for her and her new boo.

"Business as usual. KenKen got me in overdrive tryna catch up where my pops left off. After that, it's just you and me - unless you wanna bring in a third wheel like last time," Rob stated more as a suggestion.

"I aim to please, babe, so you know I'm with it," Gigi said.

"Hold up I know that ain't…" Rob started until he was sure of what he was seeing.

K-Dawg pulled up next to the gas pump and threw the truck in park. Young Mack didn't waste any time getting out because he had to piss. Without first observing his surroundings, he got out and rushed to the gas station's double doors.

"Check who finally decided to come outside with the regular people," Rob stated as he walked up to Young Mack.

"What's the bidness, Rob?" Young Mack asked, surprised to see his people.

"You tell me, homie. You dodging me or something?"

"What would I need to be dodging you for, Rob?" Young Mack asked, finally recognizing the weapon in Rob's hand.

He looked Rob over curiously before allowing his eyes to travel over to the thick tattooed shorty close behind him and the giant on their heels, all of which were showcasing a weapon of some sort.

"Rob, you got something you tryna get off your chest that I don't know about?" Young Mack asked, stepping close to him.

"You sour, nigga. You's a sour mu'fucka, you know that?" Rob spit.

"I'm not into the whole mind reading thing, money, so if it's something that got you all twisted outta shape, then you need to speak on it now. But if not, you gotta excuse me because I gotta piss."

"You tryna play me or something? Talking like you up on me, dude. If I say so, you die right here," Rob growled, filled with anger.

"Now you talking that shit I love to hear."

Rob and his crew turned to see K-Dawg's massiveness standing there clutching two golden Draco pistols with drums in both. Rob was at a loss of words and so was his crew until Pop slid through the doors of the gas station with his .50 caliber handgun aimed at K-Dawg's head.

"Not so fast, big fella!" Young Mack surprised Pop with how quick he removed the chrome FN handgun from his hip.

"Ain't no stalemates tonight if we don't want it to be." K-Dawg grinned.

"I thought we ate from the same plate, Rob?" Young Mack eyed his old friend.

"We did," Rob replied while putting his weapon away.

"I gotta be missing something here," Young Mack stated and lowered his weapon as well.

"Pop, Monsta, Gigi, let's roll!" Rob ordered without giving his explanation.

"We still need gas, bossman. You sure?" Pop inquired while keeping his eyes locked on K-Dawg, who had one of his weapons trained in his direction.

"Pump the gas then, and we out. Another time, Young Mack," Rob promised.

"You stackin yo' plate too high, li'l homie. I'm more than you can handle. I suggest you get up with me once you clear your emotions because I'm not your enemy."

"Yeah, yeah, yeah!" Rob waved him off and opened the back door for Gigi, who never turned her back to Young Mack and his henchmen.

"What's poppin', Pop. You playing chess or not?" K-Dawg teased the man with a sinister smile on his face. He loved action like this, and the two big men before him weren't scaring shit if that's what they thought.

"Hunt or be hunted, nigga!" Pop repped his shit before throwing his huge arm over his brother's shoulder and walking away from K-Dawg.

"Say that shit then, Blood!" K-Dawg yelled before stepping back to the gas pump.

Young Mack watched them closely as he moved through the store. Stepping to the counter, he spoke to the Arab man before dropping a few hundred on the counter.

"Everything good, Akh?" Mike asked, gripping his .40 cal automatic and speaking in his native language.

"All is with Allah, Akh. Just fill me up and keep the change brother."

"You got it, boss," Mike replied and did what he was ordered to do.

Young Mack couldn't believe the nuts on Rob. How could he step to him like that after he'd held him down like a brother in the streets?

"What did he mean I'm sour?" he asked himself and thought hard on it.

He knew there would be some much-needed calls to be made after what had just taken place.

Chapter 6

"Everything good?" K-Dawg asked, sitting next to Young Mack in the waiting area of the rehab that housed his mother.

Young Mack sat deep in thought. He hadn't spoken a word since the wild scene at the gas station. Everything about it irked the hell outta him and he couldn't figure out what the hell had crawled up Rob's ass and made him an enemy.

"Just wondering what's on dude's mind that would make him come at me like that. I mean, we used to eat from the same plate - not on no get rich shit, but we ate plenty, and I can't understand why he'd try my hand like that."

"I can always lay on them bitches if you want," K-Dawg offered.

"Loyalty, fam, but my focus is elsewhere right now. I know something off with him and he's holding something in, but he gon' get himself killed going about it the wrong way."

"It's your call, big homie, and you know we rockin' how you rockin' regardless. Plus, I wanna know what them boys he got with him look like on some gangsta shit," K-Dawg confessed. He'd been fiending for some kinda action with them since he set eyes on them.

"Mr. Miller," the young male clerk got his attention after stepping from behind the hallway door.

"Yeah." Young Mack stood up.

"Ms. Gaines will see you now," the man stated while holding the door open.

Young Mack hadn't seen Miley Gaines since their last run-in with each other. Miley was truly a wild and adventurous woman and he had no problem sexing her ass crazy.

"That's good, baby. Now close the door when you leave," Miley spoke motherly to the young man, who obliged her request. "I see you wanna sign your mother outta our care. Is that right?" Miley asked, keeping it professional.

"Yeah. A family emergency came about and she's very needed - no offense to your facility," Young Mack stated sincerely.

"None taken, my dear, but there are some files that need to be filled out first," Miley handed him a clipboard with a stack of documents attached to it.

"All these?" Young Mack asked with his face twisted up.

"I'm sorry, is there a problem?" she asked all business.

"Not at all," he replied, then began the paperwork.

After minutes of silence in the office, Young Mack had enough.

"Excuse me, what does this word mean?" he asked with a puzzled expression on his face.

"What word?" She looked up and lowered her glasses.

"This one." He pointed as if she could see it from across the room.

He had taken it upon himself to sit on the cushioned sofa there in her office for comfort while doing the paperwork.

Miley came from around the desk wearing a tight pinstriped skirt without hose and no shoes, showing off her perfectly pedicured feet. The white dress shirt she wore was unbuttoned to the perfect length to where he could see her black lace bra and ample cleavage. His dick hardened just from the sight of the sexy white woman.

"Which word are you referring to?" she asked while bending at his side.

"This one," Young Mack said and moved the clipboard from his lap to reveal his exposed hardness.

"Wowww, it's, uhh… Shiiit, your dick is beautiful." She couldn't control herself after seeing his hard dick - not that she wanted to either.

Unbeknownst to him, she had removed her hose and panties when he called saying he was coming over. Her juices were flowing down her creamy white thighs just from the sight of his veiny black dick.

"How about we skip the paperwork and take care of a different kind of business," Young Mack suggested while stroking his dick to its full length.

Miley tore her eyes away from his lap and stepped over to her desk. She placed her hands on her desk palms down with her head lowered. This young man was having a major effect on her womanhood.

"Why haven't you called?" she asked, fighting her own temptations.

Young Mack stood and removed his clothes. Without saying a word, he approached her from the back making sure to wedge his pole between her thick ass cheeks.

"I've been busy, Miley. I told you there's a lot of weight on my shoulders while running my family's business."

He rubbed up her back, noticing the light trail of freckles down the center, as she removed her shirt. A soft moan escaped her throat as his hands slid around her neck and gripped it with a little pressure.

"Do you forgive me?" he asked, grinding his dick against the material of her skirt where her ass cheeks separated.

"Please," she moaned, completely turned on while reaching for the hem of her skirt.

"Please what?" He licked her ear before biting her lobe and squeezing one of her breasts with his free hand. He was oblivious to her movements until he felt the material of her skirt rising.

"Tighter." She placed her hand over his around her throat. "Now fuck me hard until you make me forgive you for keeping my pussy throbbing for so long while I waited for you."

"You ain't said shit," Young Mack replied before lining the head of his shit up with her wet opening and ramming into her mercilessly.

"Holy shit!" she screamed from his forceful entry.

He worked her channel with so much force the sounds of his thighs colliding with her ass cheeks erupted into the hallway, but neither of them gave too much of a damn.

"I want Ma released within the next hour, do-you-hear-me," he growled as he pounded her middle from the back.

"Ye-ye-yes! I hear you, oh my God!" Miley stated as a tremendous climax rocked her body.

The clenching of her muscles tightened around his dick as her orgasm reached its peak making it impossible for him to hold back much longer. As her climax subsided, she continued to vigorously rub her exposed clit while he continued to deep stroke her, bringing down every wall she had put up. Of course, he didn't know what he was doing to her mental by providing her so much pleasure. He couldn't have known, she thought to herself as yet another climax approached.

"Damn, this pussy juicy and tight as fuck, ma. I'm 'bout to come hard in the white pussy!" he growled.

"I'm coming with you. Shiiit, I need your cum inside my hot pussy, baby, I need it so damn bad!"

"Say that shit then. Ahhh, here it go!"

He blasted inside her silky walls so hard it brought him to his tiptoes.

"Baby, you're in my stomach, I can feel your dick in my fucking stomach!" Miley yelled as another climax ripped through her making her knees crumble.

"Whoa," Young Mack tightened his arms around her, holding her close.

Sweat shined on her forehead, sticking hair to her face as she looked back over her shoulder at him.

"Anything you want you can have. Just never keep this dick away from me," Miley confessed.

"I hear you, ma."

"Promise me you'll always kill this pussy and I'll be yours forever."

He smiled inside at the crazy-talking woman. He knew his get down in the sack, but he'd never fucked a woman into committing her life to him.

"I promise, ma. Now get that paperwork taken care of for me."

"Don't need it. She'll be out shortly, my king." She smiled and winked at him before fixing her clothes as best as possible. She slowly made her way around her desk as he got dressed and got to work on releasing his mother.

After a few taps on her keyboard, she informed him that his mother would be released as soon as she was able to get all of her things packed. Stepping back around her desk, she stood before him in all her confidence. She stared him up and down from head to toe and knew he would be a great fit in her life, if he could prove to be trustworthy. She stepped closer into his face and spoke sternly.

"I know you're clueless as to who I really am and I won't hold that against you, but I meant every word of what I said. Just remember your promise and I'll remember mine." She stood on her tiptoes and kissed his lips before probing them with her tongue. He reluctantly allowed her access and their tongues wrestled with one another while he firmly gripped her ample booty.

"I got'chu, ma," he replied after their long kiss.

"And I got you. I'm just one phone call away, no matter the situation. I mean that," Miley confessed truthfully before heading to open the office door. "If you don't mind, would you please send my assistant in here to clean me up."

The look he gave her sealed the deal for her. She had to have him in her life, and now that she had what she hoped would be her ticket to his heart, she knew she must play her cards right.

"Don't worry, honey, he likes what you have here, not what I have here," she explained, grabbing his thick meat and putting his hand between her legs.

She had to release him because her juices were threatening to escape her pussy once again.

"It's all good," he replied in his usual calm demeanor before turning and vanishing from her presence.

He stepped into the waiting area and found K-Dawg smiling like the cat that stole the canary.

"Yo, Miley needs you," Young Mack informed the young guy at the desk.

"Ooooh, details!"

Young Mack and K-Dawg watched the young man transform right before their very eyes. K-Dawg shook his head in amazement as he stood and followed Young Mack out of the company's front office building.

"Didn't see that coming." He laughed and Young Mack agreed as they walked together. "So where to next, mister pornstar?" K-Dawg laughed while climbing behind the wheel of the Cadillac Escalade.

"Gotta stay put. Ma should be out here soon," Young Mack stated after chuckling at K-Dawg's comment.

"Ma?" K-Dawg looked confused.

"My mom's been in rehab for the last few months and now that Pops is home, he demanded that she be released and returned home."

"That's heavy, homie. I didn't know about your moms," K-Dawg sympathized with his situation.

"It's cool, gangsta. Ma's a warrior. You'll see."

Young Mack smiled as he witnessed his mother walking through the doors only minutes later. She had her head held high and he could feel an air of relief.

Sylvia was back, and seeing her son was like seeing the sun for the very first time. It brought tears to her eyes as he stepped from the dark-colored SUV. She smiled as the tears escaped her eyes and she ran into his opened arms.

"I'm back, baby, Momma back!" she cried into his chest as all kinds of emotions filled her at once.

"I know, Ma I know," Young Mack replied as he held her while fighting back tears of his own.

"I love you, baby, Momma loves you!" Sylvia stated while wiping away her tears.

"I love you too, Ma, and as much as I would love to stand here and live in this moment, we have somewhere to be and someone to see." He smiled, looking deep into her curious eyes.

"Who we going to see, Junior?"

Yep, his moms was back and he was sure of it. The only time he'd ever heard her call him Junior was during the times when she was living a clean and sober life before the collapse of their family's empire.

"Don't worry none, Ma, you'll see once we get there." He smiled and winked at K-Dawg, who instantly drove away from the rehab facility.

$$\$\$\$\$\$$$

"I should've smashed that bitch-ass nigga!" Rob yelled after taking another swig from his bottle of pure white Hennessy.

"Baby, what's going on and who was that dude? We could've handled them if you wanted," Gigi stated reassuringly.

"Didn't you see his man up them two pretty bitches?"

"Yeah, but I had a line on him before that even happened. You shouldn't sleep on me, bae. I'm way more seasoned than you realize, and so are the brothers," she admitted. She wanted desperately to explain to him the true nature of her upbringing, but she didn't wanna say anything that would jeopardize her new relationship with him, so she held her tongue.

"I bet you are, ma." He waved her off, truly sleeping on her gangsta.

She saw his blinded gesture, but decided not to hold it against him because she knew he had no idea of how deadly his own team was. Of course he didn't. His father handpicked and groomed them to carry his son to the next level and secure his legacy. Never did they ever imagine Kool losing his life before he could be handed his father's throne. Brokenhearted and knocked out of their promised empire, no one, not even Phatts, could imagine him having a son he never even knew about from the same wife that birthed the only son he'd grown to know from her womb.

"Not to pry or anything but was that the guy who got at your pops?" Gigi asked while walking on her knees to the foot of the king-sized bed, where he paced the floor back and forth.

"Yes. I mean, no. Yes and no. I don't know!" Rob said, noticing the gap between her tattooed thighs, where her juiciness sat in plain sight.

"What do you mean? It's either he did or he didn't," she replied while removing her tight-fitting T-shirt and releasing her tattooed tits with their pierced nipples.

"His call, but not by his hands." Rob squeezed his hardening crotch while eyeing her bomb-ass body.

"Doesn't matter. If he knew it was your pops, he's still in violation," she stated while removing her booty shorts and exposing her thick vaginal lips.

"Hell, I didn't even know the guy was my pops," Rob admitted while openly stroking his erection through his pants.

"Not his fault then, bae. He's a street cat, just like you, and I'm sure he had his reasons. Your pops wasn't no easy picking. You better know that," she stated, then stepped down from the bed to remove his clothes.

Once they were completely naked, she took a drink from his hard liquor before she got on her knees and engulfed his entire length down her throat, gagging only a little.

"Do that shit, ma," he appraised her head game. It turned him on a lot to see her long pornstar tongue on his dick as she took him on. "Keep on and you gon' make that mu'fucka shoot," he said, loving her warm wet mouth.

"I need to sit on this dick now," Gigi moaned while slapping his thickness against her tongue. She had two digits buried inside herself as she sucked him off. She slowly removed them and offered each of them to him, and he eagerly accepted her juicy fingers.

He sucked hard on her juicy digits, trying with everything in him to get all of her essence from them. She stood and pushed his body back hard enough for him to be seated in the love seat behind him. His tool stood tall as he slouched down in the chair, waiting for her to do her thing. She took her time straddling his lap and taking all that he had to give. She was a tough chick inside and out, but she'd never fucked a guy with as much dick as Rob. He was well over the biggest she'd ever had, and it really stretched her tight walls to the limit.

"Cumming already?" he boasted as he watched her cream load his thickness.

"Fucking right," Gigi moaned as she rose and fell on his full nine inches.

"I love how you take all that dick in this little-ass body," he spoke motivating her to just let herself go as he lifted to meet her thrust for thrust.

"I'ma make you love me, you just watch and see!" She looked back at him while gliding on him with ease. Her pussy was soaked after two quick orgasms.

"Get you, baby, this dick belongs to you, take that shit!"

She began to twerk her ass cheeks while slamming down on him with as much force as she could muster. She yelled out as yet another climax shook her equilibrium, but she didn't slow up one bit.

"Fuck, I'm 'bout to fade, ma."

Gigi bounced up and down a few more times before releasing him from her wetness. She dropped to the floor between his legs and sucked him hard until he exploded deep in her throat. She didn't waste a drop, and he delivered a lot for her to swallow.

"You got a nigga hooked already, you know that?" Rob asked as he rubbed her erect nipples.

"I hope so, because my loyalty belongs to you. I'll kill for you. I'll protect you, and I won't hesitate to die for you," she professed.

"That's a lot for someone you just met," he said, looking into her eyes.

"It's not if you know what you want."

"And what's that?" he asked curiously.

"Your full loyalty in return. I'm down for whatever you're down for in the streets and in the sheets, and all I ask for is for you to never shit on me."

"I got you, ma," he agreed.

"Can I offer you some advice, daddy?"

"Go 'head, shoot."

"I think you should talk to the guy Young Mack and feel him out. If he didn't know Phatts was your pops, you gotta figure out why he sent the hit. It's the only thing that stands between our peace and a war," Gigi jeweled him.

"You may be right, but no matter what, I know Ma is gonna want the people responsible for Pop's death. Not only that, she's rumored to have killed my brother, her son, so shit ain't gon' be that easy."

He couldn't deny how bad it felt not to be able to get to know his biological father and brother. He had to figure out what role Young Mack truly played in all of this. He was deep in thought when Monster entered his room.

"Boss, got a call from KenKen, said he couldn't reach you on your line. He also said it's important that you contact him now," Monsta said, eyeing Gigi's sexy body as she stood and covered herself in a pink silk robe.

"I'll hit him up now," Rob stated, and Monsta turned to leave the room. "Yo, Monsta!" Rob called out, stopping him in his tracks just as he was about to close the door with a huge smile on his face.

"'Sup, boss?"

"Next time knock before you enter," Rob ordered.

"The door was open, but I got you." Monsta left without another word exchanged.

Rob picked up his pants from the floor and took out his cell phone. He saw the three missed calls from KenKen and quickly hit his number back.

"Meet me behind the Beamer dealership downtown in ten minutes, and don't keep me waiting," KenKen said, clearly irritated, and then ended their call.

"Rude mu'fucka." Rob tossed his phone on top of his discarded pants and looked up to see Gigi waiting for him in the doorway of the bathroom.

"Let's shower before we roll out. I need you to cum inside this pussy this time." She smiled seductively.

"We better hurry then."

$$$$$

"You been watching your back in these streets, baby? It's sweet out here, but take it from me, son, shit ain't sugar by a long shot. Never let an unsure problem become a too late solution, you hear me?" Sylvia jeweled her only child like the old street veteran she was.

"I got'chu, Ma." Young Mack smiled because he loved the wisdom his mother delivered.

"No you don't. Baby, what's your name?" She turned her focus to K-Dawg.

"Kenneth, but everybody call me K-dawg," he replied while looking back through the rearview mirror.

"Okay, K-Dawg it is then. Bodies?"

"Like a Drake concert." He chuckled.

"Okay, anytime you see a threat coming towards my baby, slide that ass," she ordered.

"Yes ma'am," K-Dawg agreed without looking over at Young Mack.

"Ma, you can't be issuing orders like that to my men. You're not even in the game anymore," Young Mack protested.

"Honey," Sylvia sang playfully, pinching his cheek. "I am the game," she spoke with finality.

Young Mack shook his head at his mother. Part of him wanted to take it to Rob and his new little crew for rolling up on him like shit was really sweet. Another part of him wanted desperately to know where the blatant act of disrespect was stemming from. To top it all off, it's like his mother could see right through his thoughts.

"Nigga drew heat, big homie," K-Dawg stated as if he, too, was a damn mind reader.

"That's the sad part." Young Mack knew what he was getting at.

He also knew that his mother always knew when something was bothering him, so it was final. One way or another, Rob had to pay severely for their acts of transgression.

"Junior, umm, why are we here and whose cars are those?" Sylvia asked, utterly confused.

"It's a surprise celebration, Ma." Young Mack smiled.

"But you pulled me out before I graduated," she stated while still puzzled.

"Doesn't matter, Ma. You are a queen either way and I love you."

"I love you too, baby!" Sylvia's eyes misted over as the vehicle pulled up to their home's front door.

It had been years since she last laid eyes on their family home. Just seeing it made her heart hurt and her soul smile simultaneously. She grew lightheaded once her son stepped out and opened the car door for her.

"Small turn out, huh?" She laughed, eyeing a fresh-looking Mercedes Benz C63 Coupe and a matte black Chevy Tahoe.

"Only the ones that matter most." Young Mack smiled and kissed his mother's cheek before leading her to the front door.

As she walked up the few concrete steps leading up to the huge front door to their home, locks could be heard as they unlatched from the door frame before the door was snatched open. Sylvia couldn't believe her eyes. It couldn't be. Her mind had to be playing games with her.

"Hello, my queen," Mackmillions said, welcoming his woman home with open arms.

"But howww?" Sylvia stood there shocked, eyes bugged out to the max.

"It's me, love." Mackmillions stepped closer.

"I'm not high, you know. Of course it's you."

They all had to laugh at that.

"Come here." Mackmillions enveloped her small frame and drowned her in his embrace.

"We got a lot of work to do, my love," Sylvia stated as the tears began to fall, soaking up his shirt.

"Don't I know it," Mackmillions agreed while eyeing the unmarked car fifty yards down the block.

Chapter 7

Smoke filled the cabin of KenKen's Range Rover as he sat quietly in thought while waiting for his new protégé to arrive. He watched from the windshield as the stage was being set and couldn't hide the sinister grin on his face. Nearly half an hour passed before Rob showed up with his crew all dressed in black from head to toe. He smiled at the assemble of characters because he liked what he saw in them.

"What's the bidness, Ken?" Rob asked curiously as KenKen stepped out of his truck, which was sitting on chrome twenty-six-inch Forgies, and gave him a pound.

"Got a situation for you," KenKen stated, then tapped the hood of his truck, and the bright headlights illuminated the wall before them.

"Damn, my nigga KenKen on his savage shit out here!" Monsta exclaimed, filled with hype.

"Shut up, fool!" Pop scolded his little brother.

"Nawl, Monsta, my guy, this is y'all's problem," KenKen stated as he leaned back against the front of his ride.

"Wait, what you mean it's our problem? We ain't no cleaning crew," Rob spoke up with a menacing expression before KenKen cut him off.

"He's been missing ever since your pops left us."

"Elaborate," Rob requested.

"I've went over the books, and he's in the hole with your father for a cool million dollars. None of that belongs to the

Realm, so like I said, this is entirely your problem," KenKen concluded, then took a deep drag from his kush-filled blunt.

Rob understood exactly where this was headed, so he immediately jumped into action.

"Yo, snatch this pussy down!" he ordered, and Pop did the honors. "Tape." Rob ordered the tape to be removed from the victim's mouth, and Monsta painfully snatched it away from the guy's already bruised mouth. He also had a bruised eye that was swollen shut from an obvious beating.

"What's your name, fam?" Rob asked the guy at his feet.

"Tony. Fuck all this shit, man. I told that nigga I can get the money."

"Wise advice, T. Only speak when you're asked to," Rob stated after delivering a heavy blow to the injured man's good eye. "Now that we have an understanding, I need to know how you're gonna get me my money?"

"It's already on deck, my dude," Tony assured.

"So what did you do for my people to chain yo' ass to a damn wall like that?" Rob chuckled and so did Monsta.

"Man, fuck KenKen! Bitch-ass nigga got anger issues but can't punch worth shit. That's why he let his goons do his dirty work." Tony spit towards KenKen's Italian loafers.

"Whoa, this nigga bold as shit, ain't he?" Rob laughed, looking in Gigi's direction. He could see the thirst for blood through the portals of her soul.

"Okay, let's cut all the chat. Where's my money, Tony?" Rob asked sternly.

"At my house, like I've been tryna tell this asshole since they started wilding on me."

"And home is where? Nigga, stop stalling and tell me how to get my fuckin' bread."

Rob was growing tired of all the talking and little did he know, he definitely wasn't the only one.

Boom!

Rob jumped from the loud roar of someone's weapon going off. The reflex caused him to shut his eyes and when he opened them, blood and brains were mixing together to create a thick mist in the air. He heard the sound of Tony's body slump to the ground before he actually saw it. Rob looked first to KenKen, who nonchalantly blew out a huge cloud of smoke as he looked on, nodding his approval at the sight of Tony's dead body. His eyes then traveled towards his crew. He locked eyes with Gigi, and his face instantly twisted up as she gave him a shrug of her shoulders.

"Who told you to do that?" he scolded her.

"I already know where he lives, and I know his bitch, so getting the money will be easy. But bae, you were talking to him too much."

Rob nodded his head, clearly annoyed, before ordering his men to dump the dead man in the dumpster next to where he laid.

"Get at me once you get settled for the night. I got big plans for you, kid," KenKen stated from the back seat of his truck before the window rose and the truck took off.

Rob's blood boiled as he rode home with his team. Nothing pissed him off more than a needy bitch other than a bitch who didn't seem to recognize her place. He knew he had to put his foot down because Gigi was clearly a murderous mu'fucka, and he couldn't be soft with her. After they pulled into the driveway of his modest new two-story home, he instructed Pop not to enter the garage. Pop did as requested, then shut the engine off.

"Get out," Rob ordered Pop and Monsta, who looked puzzled.

He looked at Gigi sitting next to him in the back seat wearing a questionable expression. He quickly delivered a shocking blow to her left eye with his right hand. She yelped in pain and nearly thought of hitting him back from reflex, but decided against it and reached for her aching eye.

"I said get the fuck out!" he yelled before driving a left hook deep into Gigi's rib cage.

"Ahhh fuck!" she cried out after another surprising blow.

"You wanna be the man, bitch? Grow a dick. But until then, you better respect your position beside me or get put the fuck behind me!" Rob growled after releasing the pressure he was applying with both hands around her throat.

Gigi gasped for air in big gulps as her lungs refilled and flexed, causing her ribs to ache more.

"Do we understand each other? Because you can step now if that's your choice," Rob asked while keeping a tight grip on his pistol with his left hand in case she chose wrong.

Gigi really didn't want any smoke with her man and she knew she had messed up royally, so she nodded her head without looking him in his eyes. He reached over, causing her to flinch. After she settled, he reached and removed her hand from her eye. It had begun to swell already, but he knew she could take the pain. Still holding her wrist, he pulled her to him and kissed her bruised eye. Even though he was a bit disappointed with her, he knew that he already had feelings for her and would give her the world if it was in his power. She was tense at first, but relaxed after realizing he was done with the dumb shit.

"I'm sorry, daddy, I didn't mean to overstep. I just didn't wanna hear him disrespect you like he was doing KenKen," she apologized.

"That's old news now. Just don't ever take it upon yourself to make calls unless I green light that shit. I'm not gonna be soft on you just because I think you're a bad bitch and you make this dick spit at will. At the same time, I ain't no pimp type mu'fucka to be putting my hands on you every time you fuck up either. This time was a lesson taught, and learned next time I'll knock yo' brains through this pretty-ass face of yours," Rob promised.

"Won't be a next time," Gigi submitted as she felt her kitty begin to stir.

She loved that gangsta shit, and even though she never approved of a man putting his hands on her, she'd been through way worse than what he issued out and she respected him for putting her in her place instead of allowing her to run him over.

"I pray that it won't, because I'd hate to lose you. Now enough talking, ma. Go get daddy's money," Rob chuckled as he rubbed her juicy ass cheek.

They climbed out of the back seat, he opened the driver's door for her, and she entered behind the wheel.

"Baby, I'm horny."

"Business first, ma. Call me if you have any complications, and don't dead shit unless you have to."

"I got it."

"Oh, and once she does give you the bread, dead the hoe on GP, just because I hit you."

Gigi chuckled a bit while still feeling the tenderness in her face and ribs.

"Done," she agreed before starting the car and backing out of the driveway.

Rob turned to look at his henchmen, who were already staring at him.

"So what I punched the bitch a few times? I'm fucking her. But if one of y'all ever try to undermine me like she did, I'm deading both of y'all big asses." Rob pointed at them father-like.

"We got'chu, big fella." Monsta chuckled and received a quick elbow to his side from his big brother. "Fuck you do that for?"

"Everything is over stood, big homie. My li'l brother just got a fucked-up sense of humor," Pop spoke up.

"But he already know that shit," Monsta whined.

"Shut up." Pop waved him off as they entered the house behind Rob, who was shaking his head at the both of them.

"Bro, you gotta let me get my lick back because you tryna make me look bad," Monsta stated.

"You're six foot four and weight over three hundred pounds. You already look bad for a twenty-year-old."

"Hater," Monsta replied and left the situation alone.

$$$$$

"Something big is going on and these mu'fuckas tryna treat us like some damn beat cops," Chandler fumed as he paced back and forth inside the basement of his partner's home.

"You buggin', bruh, but check this shit out. Why can't we just go ahead and enjoy these two days off? We could call up some bitches from Colorado's and chill the fuck out." Drexler could already picture them having a blast with a few stripper broads for the night.

"Fuck all that, kid, our lives could be at stake here. Then you talkin' 'bout real live pussy like your ol' lady ain't up the fuck there. Fuck she gon' think about all that?"

"Man, I tell my ol' lady we got liquor and pussy down here and she'll be the first one to start throwing money." Drexler laughed, but was serious as shit. "On top of that, bruh, have you gotten any pussy since you been down south?"

"Damn, what are you, the dick detective or sum'n?"

"I didn't think so. I'm calling my li'l bitch and she 'bout to bring whoever through. Nigga, you 'bout to get some of this sweet-ass down south pussy!"

Drexler did just as he said he would and shit got popping as soon as those bitches hit the basement.

With everything going on around them, Chandler wasn't at all comfortable with their situation, but he knew his partner was right for a change. He needed to spend some time relaxing and forgetting about work for a minute, so he decided to get himself a taste of the sweet down south pussy his partner had just put on his plate.

"Fuck it, might as well rock out."

Drexler went crazy upon hearing that.

$$$$$

Mr. Mackmillions hadn't felt so complete since the night before his arrest over a decade ago. He'd lost it all after falling victim to someone in his circle of power player's deceit. Nothing could have readied him for his fall at the time it had come for him. Everyone disappeared and not one person from his inner circle of power came to aid or assist him in his situation. For years, he thought his associates were tryna play it safe by keeping their distance from his highly publicized drama with the Feds. It wasn't until the many failed attempts on his life that he figured out that the power and influence had shifted amongst them. Everything he'd worked so hard to build had fallen apart with him on the outs, and nothing would remain the same.

Sylvia shuffled a bit before finding comfort in his arms as she slept. The mere sight of her made his heart pound his chest. Having her back in his life and being able to touch her in ways he only was able to dream about for over a decade was more than he could ask for, and he welcomed it with pride. He had his home back, thanks to his son's incredible devotion to his parents. He had his family back and his right-hand man slept only feet away from his room in one of their many guest rooms. Em stayed on his mind, yet he hadn't reached out to her since his return. He made a mental note to get up with her as soon as he made clear of some free time. He kissed his wife, earning a moan in return.

"Something on my mind, babe. I need to step out and talk to Max," he whispered in her ear before planting another kiss on her lips.

"I understand, bae, just don't be long," she replied, and with that he was up and dressed before stepping into the guest room, ready to wake Max from his sleep.

"Waitin' on you, brudda." Max surprised him as he stepped into the doorway.

"Thought you'd be asleep."

"Been d'ere already, na I'm ready to get me life ba'k," Max shot back.

"Let's go. We got a lot to do."

The duo stepped out of Mackmillions' six-million-dollar mansion and into his eight-car garage, where all of his toys remained.

"We gotta knock some dust off these old thangs, Max." Mackmillions smiled while selecting a set of keys from his key rack.

"No time like dee present." Max nodded and caught the keys to Mackmillions' customized '69 Camareo.

These visits are long past due, he thought to himself as they pulled from the door of the garage.

After realizing that there was no unmarked vehicle up the block from his home, he smiled and knew tonight would be the first step in regaining the life he left behind so many years ago.

$ $ $ $ $

Fifteen minutes passed before Max brought the car to a stop fifty yards up the block in the very quiet and modest subdivision in southwest Houston.

"We're 'ere." Max nudged Mackmillions once he killed the engine.

"I have to say, Max, I expected more from this one."

"Ye kno' he neva had dee heart to stand for himself."

"Yeah, I know." Mackmillions sighed as he exited the car with Max close behind.

Darkness surrounded the blocks of the tight knit neighborhood watch area like a cloak. Mackmillions read the white and blue signs with the big eyeball on them and knew they had to be very careful not to alert any unwanted attention, or the place would quickly be surrounded by the boys in blue.

"Get us in, Max," Mackmillions ordered, and Max took off down the side of the two-story brick home.

Mackmillions stood quietly squared off with the wall in front of the main entrance and waited. After hearing the locks slowly turn on the big wooden door, Mackmillions checked his watch before entering.

"You've slowed up a bit." He smiled at Max.

"No tools for tee alarm couldn't fry circuit, so we must hurry."

"Don't worry yourself. We'll be good," Mackmillions assured.

Stepping into the cool foyer of the home calmed Mackmillions more then he wanted to be.

Guess all that training paid off, he thought to himself, bringing back to mind the lessons with Shadow.

Thinking of Shadow brought back thoughts of the mission he'd accepted once things were squared away with regaining his freedom.

Shadow had friends in very high places and the things he was able to bring to light only brought about another level of respect in Mackmillions that only extended towards his son and Max. His relationship with his beast of a cousin surpassed any and couldn't be measured to none. Shadow made his mark and provided all that he said he would for Mackmillions to embark on a journey that could change life for the both of them, and Mackmillions was a man of his word in all ways.

After carefully searching the first floor of the modestly furnished home, it was time to take it up the stairs, where a muffled sound could be heard vibrating off the walls of the hallway. After clearing the stairs, Mackmillions and Max both made their way towards the unmistakable sound coming from one of the bedrooms. They thoroughly checked the occupants of the first three bedrooms and were certain that none of them were the one person they'd come for.

Mackmillions moved with the stealth of a phantom into the last room while never taking his eyes off his mark.

John Thomilson jumped out of his sleep, traumatized by one hell of a nightmare. He looked both ways as he tried to steady his panicked breathing while perspiration coated his smoothly-shaven face.

"Honey, are you okay?" his wife, Evangelinr, asked after waking from his sudden movements.

"Sure, just need a cold drink of water, if you don't mind."

"Oh no, I don't mind at all, sweetie, just hurry back."

Eva wasn't the one, and her husband already knew what was up, but she had to admit that it was a nice try though.

"I meant…"

"I know exactly what you meant," she shut him down before turning over with her back to him. She wasn't in favor of him disturbing her sleep.

"You still trippin' 'bout the game, I see. Just accept that your Cowboys suck and you should probably find another team to give your unwavering loyalty to, like my Eagles." He chuckled after not getting a witty come back and swung his legs out of bed.

Just as his feet fell into the comfort of his house slippers, a sudden chill overcame him as he stared into the darkened corner of his bedroom. He wasn't sure if anything was there, but it felt as if something or someone was there lying in wait. He slowly climbed to his feet on uneasy limbs. His legs only carried him so fast as he nervously made his way to the room's light switch. He rushed to turn on the light once he reached it, but nothing happened. Over and over he tried again, only to get the same results.

"That's weird," he spoke softly to no one in particular. He decided that he was probably tripping and just forgot to change the light bulb, one of many things his wife stayed in his ass about. He made his way out of the room and slowly down the hallway, where he spotted the soft glow coming from each of his three daughter's bedrooms from their night lights. "Yeah, light bulb," he convinced himself and chuckled.

The illuminating lights helped calm his heightened nerves as he moved down the stairs and made his way into the dark kitchen. Entering the doorway, John flipped the lights on and immediately realized he loved the darkness that spooked him more than the image of the man he'd been running from in his nightmares standing there at his kitchen's island.

"I warned you of my coming, John," Mackmillions stated, never losing eye contact with the petrified man.

"You...my dreams...you said that in my nightmares," John stammered through his shaking words.

"I know, but the only thing now is for you to explain to me why I'm here rather than being in bed with my lovely wife."

John hated the day he was dragged into Miller's situation. He absolutely hated it then and he hated it now. Mackmillions had always been a stellar player in their business dealings, and John had no reason to show any disloyalty to the underworld giant.

"Dub, they forced me." John's words came out as nothing more than a whisper as his chin hit his chest in total defeat.

"Dub?" Mackmillions asked curiously.

"It's short for double 'em. A name I've always called you," John explained.

"Has a nice ring to it," Mackmillions stated before removing his weapon from his hip. "John, there are two things I need from you more than I've needed anything in my life."

Hearing a glimmer of hope radiating from Mackmillions' voice made John look him in the eyes.

"First, the code to your security system."

"Ten-twenty-six-twelve-zero-four-pound."

The chirping sound of the numbers being entered into the keypad of his home security system both shocked and terrified him at once. Piss threatened to escape his bladder.

"Secondly, I need to know everything and everyone, leave nothing out. If I get the feeling that you're holding out or that you're somehow being untruthful, your daughters die one by one, then your wife while I make you watch. Then and only then will I relieve you of your life with my bare hands," Mackmillions promised before resting his weapon on the kitchen island.

"It was so long ago, Mack, how could I possibly remember all of that?" John protested weakly.

"Honey, what's going on?" Evangeline asked with a broken voice and tears cascading down her cheeks as Max led her into the kitchen at gunpoint.

"Come on, man, my family will die if I tell you anything. Mack, have some compassion," John whined.

"Evangeline, is it?" Mackmillions asked, turning his attention to John's beautiful Hispanic wife.

"Yes. Please don't hurt us, whoever you are," she begged with a wet face from all the tears she shed.

"Evangeline, I'm only an animal when people like your husband do things to me that'll make me hunt them down. Now let me ask you this. You love him?"

"Yes, with all of my heart," she replied truthfully.

"In that case, would you mind making us fellas some fresh blueberry waffles, heavy on the butter with extra syrup for me and my guy. I'm sure you already know what your husband likes." Mack shocked them with his request.

"Yes, anything you want, just don't hurt us." She immediately began to shuffle around the kitchen in haste to comply to his demands.

"Now let's see if you love your wife as much as she clearly loves you. Let's start from the very first time someone reached out to you with the intent to take me down." Mackmillions leaned against the kitchen island, eager to hear everything he knew John would reveal.

$ $ $ $ $

KenKen spit out the window of his truck once he saw his personal line light up with a number he dreaded answering. The fact that he never had an option in the fact steamed him to his core because he always loved to look at himself as his own boss, but for years now, shit just wasn't feeling as kosher as he was accustomed to.

"Yeah," he answered dryly once he accepted the call.

"So, how's our latest recruit taking to the vast open waters out there?" the voice came through from the other end.

"Everything's peachy, and as long as I'm guiding him, I'm pretty sure it'll stay that way," KenKen replied arrogantly.

"That's good; very good. You know, KenKen, it's not often that you blacks help each other out, so I have to say this."

KenKen's jaw muscles flexed at the blatant line of disrespect, but he knew there was nothing he could do yet.

"You let this one die, you die with him."

KenKen's phone beeped, indicating that the call had ended, much to his pleasure. He couldn't believe this man was the head chair of the Realm and coming outta pocket like that. For something he had sworn his life to loyally represent, he wasn't feeling at all comfortable with that decision these days. KenKen was under the old street creed, "Death Before Dishonor", and never backed out of agreements he'd made with blood signings. But never had he bent over backwards for someone else's personal gain and his displeasure. Since the change in power too many years ago to count, he knew the day would come where he'd have to reassess how he did things.

"We'll see about that, mu'fucka!" he said aloud to no one in particular as his mind started thinking of ways to take out the top dog of the underworld.

Chapter 8

Ambrea sat entranced as she watched the exuberant rays from the morning sun harass the grassy mountain sides while fighting its way up over the mountaintops. Her mind boggled with the entirety of their situation. She looked over and saw Young Mack, who was smiling as he binge-watched rerun episodes of the comedy show *Martin* as if he didn't have a care in the world. She hated herself for feeling so strongly about him and loving the man that he had grown to be over the years. Being honest, he was way more than she ever thought he'd amount to being. Their relationship was uniquely special and designed by them both. The attraction between the two dated back to their first meet and was parallel to none. Ambrea had always been in relationships off and on separate from what she shared with him, and with her being the older of the two, she didn't want him falling in love with her after she first put the pussy on him. In the end, she couldn't believe how majorly she'd misjudged him. Young Mack had grown to be everything she could ever want in a man, but she guessed life hadn't meant for them to be anything more than what they were to each other: lovers and nothing more.

Young Mack was indeed his father's son when it came to most things in life and definitely when it came to how he treated his women. Taking pages straight outta his pops' handbook, he learned very valuable life lessons. Their sex life was nothing short of amazing, and Young Mack never made her feel uncomfortable in their relationship. His loyalty never wavered. He was a true Boy Scout, to say the least. Everything was kosher until the night he made her climax more times in one session than any of her other boyfriends had ever accomplished altogether. After that night, she knew she was hooked, and he treated her with class, often laughed with her, didn't mind spending unscheduled time with her, and was always one to spoil her with expensive gifts, even though she could afford to buy those things herself. Thinking of all those things about him had her heart pounding hard against her chest. She'd fallen in love with a man who she'd made promise never to fall in love with her. Now their relationship was threatening to become the most dreaded nightmare if it got back to her kingpin husband.

"'Bre, snap out of it, ma, we're here." Young Mack shook her after his second time calling out to her.

"Oh, I'm sorry, I was in my own little world for a minute," she nervously laughed it off.

"Yeah, well don't be getting yourself all worked up, cuz I brought some bands with me to pay this chick off immediately, and with a low-paying job as a cleaning lady, I'm sure she'll comply," Young Mack assured her.

After exiting the rented private jet, Ambrea noticed someone standing inside the darkened hangar far ahead of them. Since their vehicle waited for them, she chalked it up as mere paranoia. Young Mack waited outside the back passenger door for her to climb in and he got in behind her before the chauffeur closed them in safely.

"Always the perfect gentleman." She shook her head at how much he affected her effortlessly.

He smiled to himself because he could always tell when she was thinking about him, even at times when her mouth wouldn't say so. That coupled with the fact that she subconsciously reached over and held his hand while staring outside at the city moving past them was a clear indication of just that. He was loving the scene here in Mexico. He'd never been there before, but always knew he wanted to make that trip. After this ordeal was in the bag, he definitely wanted to do some touring and shopping before they left for home.

The market type vibe soon vanished as they moved through miles of tall trees lining both sides of the road, providing privacy for some of the most beautiful villas he'd ever laid eyes on. Money was clearly in these developed neighborhoods, and he was sure that not just anyone could occupy those places unless they were of some major importance. The vehicle slowed down as it ran down a long path with what had to be the biggest of all the homes they had seen coming to into view.

"I think you may have the wrong address, sir," Ambrea spoke to the driver in Spanish.

He said a few words in response before she sat back and looked into Young Mack's eyes.

"What's poppin', ma, what got you all bugged out? She probably works here too."

Ambrea took a deep breath as the front gate split down the middle and granted them passage. The road ended in a circular driveway at what looked to be the entrance of the huge home. The driver pulled around to the front door, and Ambrea looked out behind them and saw a black SUV pulling in right on their behind. The windows came down and she caught a good glimpse of the driver of that vehicle as she and Young Mack climbed from the back of their ride.

"Mack, that dude followed us from the strip," she whispered, not wanting anyone to know what she saw.

"Yeah, I noticed that too," he replied as he watched their surroundings. Her dead serious stare almost made him laugh out loud as they were being escorted around to the back of the mansion. "I didn't wanna bug you out more than you already were, but know that I'm always watching and paying attention to everything."

"Like these armed guards all around us…bitch must do some helluva cleaning with hands of gold or something."

Young Mack laughed at her humorous statement before the backyard came into their full view. He immediately noticed the feminine shape of a woman swimming underwater in the crystal-clear pool. He followed her with his eyes as they walked alongside the fancy pool to a table set with drinks, where two armed guards stood posted with automatic assault rifles. The two were searched, then ordered to take their seats at the table, where they waited for the unknown.

"This is absolutely crazy," Ambrea stated as her leg bounced and her expensive red bottomed heels tapped the ground.

"Calm down. You're starting to make me nervous." Young Mack mustered a weak smile while rubbing his hand soothingly on her shaking leg.

"Oh my God, that's her." Ambrea stared at the beautiful woman climbing from the swimming pool, where one of the guards handed her a dry towel.

"Don't look like no cleaning woman to me."

"This shit is crazier than I thought," Ambrea mumbled as the woman made her way towards them. She stood as the fake cleaning lady approached with a half-smile. Her walk was that of a very confident woman, and her beauty rivaled that of Ambrea's own.

"Hi, I'm Ambrea," she began, but was cut short.

"Believe me, I know who you are, but it's him I'm interested in right now."

"Damn, straightforward and to the point, I like that. But unfortunately, this isn't a social visit. I'm here to offer you fifty thousand for the videos," Young Mack stated without standing as he tossed a Gucci bag filled with thousand-dollar bundles at her feet.

"I'll charge that disrespect to your ignorance in not knowing who you're dealing with."

"And who are we dealing with? Because our understanding was that we were coming out to meet a nice cleaning woman," Ambrea interrupted her before she could continue going in on Young Mack. She also hated the way this woman was openly ogling Young Mack.

"My name is Stephanie Valdez," the woman stated proudly.

"The cleaning lady?" Ambrea asked in full sarcasm. Stephanie chuckled a bit at the ironic look in Ambrea's eyes. It was really priceless.

"I apologize for your wrongful assessment of me, but I am no cleaning woman," Stephanie stretched her arms out and looked around her arrogantly. "Truth is, I was there to kill your husband, cut his head off, then bring it home to my Bordeaux for a play toy."

"You bitch!" Ambrea growled in anger.

"Don't be ungrateful. I let you live once, but if you ever show me your disrespect again, my kindness will be me burning your pretty little ass alive and watching your body turn to ash." The serious expression on Stephanie's face brought about a chill to Ambrea's core.

"You taking the bread or not, ma? I really got shit to tend to outside of this." Young Mack smiled while listening to the dangerous woman Stephanie.

"At last, a smile," Stephanie smiled back flirtatiously.

"You are very handsome, you know."

"I guess." Young Mack sat back and busied himself with his social media page, feigning irritation. He was really enjoying the special attention.

"Why don't we stop the games and get down to the reason we are here?" Ambrea stated. She was growing irritated herself by Stephanie's voice altogether now.

"Shall we?" Stephanie stood up, purposely dropping her towel from her perfectly sculpted body before stepping up to Young Mack and blocking Ambrea's view of him.

"Nothing on that phone could be more interesting than all of this." She moved her perfectly manicured hands softly over her Coke bottle curves, DD tits, down to her flat six pack stomach, then around her small waist, where they rested. His eyes stayed glued to her body. She was definitely killing the black Norma Kamalie bodysuit.

"Business," Young Mack suggested and stood.

Stephanie adored his handsomely good looks, and she even loved his casual and expensive taste in designer threads, but nothing captivated her more than seeing his sex game in action. She'd watched him sex Ambrea into a near euphoric coma. The things he did to her to push her over the edge, the positions he'd compelled her body to perform while applying maximized pressure, had Stephanie's pussy drenched just being in his presence. The wetness of her bathing suit concealed her arousal - not that she'd cared at all if he saw it.

"Business it is - for now." She winked and seductively licked her lips as she brushed past him, careful to add extra sway to her hips so that her ass would look even more amazing as he walked behind her.

Young Mack shook his head at all the dirty thoughts he was having of him sexing the spicy Latina woman. Truth was, he was strictly trying to remain professional in a desperate attempt not to embarrass or make Ambrea feel jealous. She wasn't his woman, but he still cared for her feelings.

Walking through the huge mansion behind Stephanie, they took in the décor of the awe-inspiring place. The expensive paintings were definitely eye-catching as well as her massive collection of hand-potted vases from her native culture. The all-white furniture looked like it belonged inside one of Oprah's mega mansions. He was sure it was expensive, along with the ultra-soft white fur rug. Stephanie took a seat and signaled for the pair to remove their shoes before stepping on the rug. She waited for them to be seated before whistling to the armed guard, who stood post ten feet away from them with his back to them, watching the front of the house. He then turned and came to her. She whispered her orders, and he immediately pulled out his phone before moving back into his position with it glued to his ear.

"My brothers shall be here soon for you," she spoke to Ambrea, then turned her gazing hazels to Young Mack. "You still haven't told me your name. Seems unfair to me now that you know mine and I've clearly invited you into my home."

Young Mack stared into her seductive eyes from where he sat next to Ambrea. Stephanie was a daring woman, and he had to admit that she was getting to him in ways he had not planned to let her.

"Mackentosh Miller the second, but everyone calls me Young Mack, or Mack for short."

"So, Young Mack, what is it that you do in life besides please women?" Stephanie uncrossed then crossed her legs while fingering the ends of her long blonde-streaked hair.

"Chess," he replied with a wink.

"Chess? Like the game of chess?"

"Yes, only I play the game of life on many different levels," he confessed through his own life's philosophy.

"Some levels enjoyed more than others, perhaps?" She was curious as to how she could implement his life only to have him destroy her in bed.

"Give or take," he admitted.

"Drugs?"

"Lucky assumption," he nodded with a smile not big enough to signal his comfort with their conversation though.

"Educated assumption, Mackentosh." She smiled exuberantly.

"How so?" he questioned.

"You're fucking the brain cells out of a kingpin's wife, so it's only safe to say that he's your coke connect. But what beats me is, how are you still paying for them if you're providing his wife with such tremendous pleasure?"

Stephanie's devilish grin told Ambrea that the comment was really directed at her.

"Look, lady, mind your fucking business and stay outta mine." Ambrea rolled her eyes, but Stephanie paid her no mind.

Young Mack sat back and eyed the beautiful woman across from him. She was definitely not as dumb as she was rich. She was seductive and classy, yet seemed adventurous and like a downright demon in bed. As much as he loved partaking in their chat, the question still remained: what were they doing there if she clearly didn't need or desire any hush money for their secret?

"You're absolutely right about that, but you know I play this game of life on——"

"Many different levels." Stephanie smiled after finishing his sentence. It wasn't hard because he'd just told her the same thing.

Ambrea sat heated about their little back and forth when he should have been trying to figure out what they were there for. His calmness in their situation made her question if he even cared about it at all. Stephanie had informed her of her brothers, obviously other enemies of her husband. They were on their way there to do God knows what with her and no telling what they would do with him, yet he still kept his cool, and she didn't know how he was doing it.

"Young Mack, these people are dangerous and you're sitting here exposing yourself to this venomous snake," Ambrea whispered in his ear.

"Now that I'm an open book and we've acquainted ourselves, are those drinks still available while we wait?" Young Mack decided to play into the fact that even though she was a rich, powerful woman, she wanted to impress him.

"Sure. What will you have?" Stephanie smiled, understanding his request for a little privacy.

"An educated guess," he replied, challenging her.

"And you?" Stephanie looked to Ambrea.

"Bottled water, thank you," Ambrea stated. She wasn't about to trust the lady to make her anything with an open lid.

"Scared I may poison you, mami?"

Young Mack laughed on the inside at the audacious woman. He loved this crazy bitch, but would never admit to anything like that. Ambrea replied without words, but with a slight shrug of her shoulder, she brought about a reaction from Stephanie before she stood and walked away. Young Mack waited until Stephanie was out of earshot before he turned to Ambrea, who was seemingly nervous about their fates.

"Bre, you gotta calm down and gain control over your emotions," he said while touching her chin and bringing her face to his own. He kissed her lips tenderly once, then twice more before releasing her. He felt Stephanie's gaze burning into the side of his face and knew those kisses would make her come for him harder than she already had.

"I just don't know what to make of this shit, Young Mack, and these people are Gurdo's enemies. I can't fathom why they want us here and why they haven't tried hurting us to get to him." She was a nervous wreck on the inside, but she'd always been one to shield her emotions from the outside world, creating a tougher shell than most could not penetrate. Even though she prayed for the best in this situation, she still didn't know what to expect.

"We'll be fine, ma. She's told me a lot more then what her mouth has admitted."

"What?" Ambrea asked, thinking that his mind was in the gutter.

"This is a very dangerous woman, and the fact that she was able to get past Gurdo's security and into close quarters with his queen and let you live, she obviously somehow saw an angle and wanted to exploit it. Now her brothers could be a lot worse than her, but females tend to be better at savagery than men especially when there is an eminent threat." Young Mack smiled and Ambrea rolled her eyes because she knew what he was getting at. "She's obviously into me, thanks to your little sex tape collection of us."

"Don't go there." Ambrea couldn't blame Stephanie Valdez after realizing what her motivation for gloating over Young Mack was.

"Plus if they wanted us dead, we'd be tied up and hanging from a ceiling in one of their warehouses."

"Makes sense." Ambrea exhaled and dropped her head on his shoulder.

"There's a nursery upstairs for my niece, if you would like a cradle for rest," Stephanie stated as she walked over with a tray of drinks.

"Sorry, but I nurse differently," Ambrea stated with an air of confidence before grabbing Young Mack's crotch. His eyes grew to the size of saucers from Ambrea's dominant stance and brazen display of sexual conduct.

"Your husband not big enough, no?" Stephanie shot back.

"What can I say? I'm spoiled," Ambrea smiled, then sipped her water.

Stephanie's eyes lowered into slits as she thought about the many ways to destroy the bitch across from her. She wasn't used to being put in her place, and women were scared to stand up to her and never disrespected her without harsh and fatal repercussions. She made a promise to herself to crash Ambrea's life with or without her brother's approval. After all, she was their enemy by association.

"So, Stephanie, you wanna hip me to what's going on? Because I thought this was a meeting about those videos." Young Mack leaned forward, giving her acknowledgement that she had his full attention, a move he learned from his father.

"It was set up for it to feel that way to motivate you two to make this trip willingly. My brothers saw my vision once I decided that she would be worth more to our cause alive than dead after I found what was on her phone."

"So what now? What's your vision?"

Products Of The Streets 2 | Demonde "Money" Anderson

"Advantage." Stephanie smiled at Ambrea, who wore a look of displeasure with the entire situation. "We know all about her role in Gurdo's operations, and since he's proven himself to be more than just another common thug who was granted Poppa's multimillion dollar company like we figured he'd be, she'll be our point of entry."

"Fuck makes you think I would help you take my husband down?" Ambrea had a strong distaste for Stephanie and her bully antics.

"Because outside of these sex tapes, your life and the lives of your loved ones are counting on you too," a male's voice sounded and garnered all of their attention.

$ $ $ $ $

Rob rolled over in bed at the sound of his blaring phone. He reached over to his nightstand and picked it up, then checked to see who the caller was before answering it immediately.

"Hey Ma, what's up?" He sounded groggy from his broken sleep.

"Nothing much. Just calling to check up on you since I haven't heard from you."

Rob sighed and immediately felt guilty for not dropping in to check her since he'd gotten his new place, a place his father owned that wasn't the property of The Realm. Whoever the hell they were, it was mystery to him.

"Sorry about that, Ma. KenKen been having me all kinds of busy keeping up with Dad's stuff."

Mary smiled after hearing him refer to her late husband as his dad. She knew all too well that he never got a chance to know him as his biological father, but to hear his acceptance of him as his father made her joyful. "Well, how about you come on over and spend some time with your old mother, and we'll share a nice dinner together?"

"Just hearing that got my stomach rumbling, Ma. You know I'm there." He smiled to himself.

"The food shall be ready by seven."

"I'm there, Ma. I love you."

"I love you too, son," Mary stated as she let a lone tear escape her water-filled eyes before ending their call. She loved her son so much, and the fact that he had to grow up through life without her and his father made her love him even more.

Rob finished the call with his mother and looked to the foot of his bed at the duffle bag filled with money. The running water in the shower let him know Gianna was there, so he got up to join her. Stepping into the bathroom, he could see her silhouette inside the shower through the misted glass shower walls. He dropped the Houston Rockets Ethika briefs he had on and slipped into the shower behind her. Gianna's body was cold. She was strapped, and he loved her sexy curves, but even more, he loved filtering through her maze of body ink. Her entire body was covered with expensive displays of tattooed artwork and he loved it. He turned her around to face him and took a look at her face where he'd struck her. The bruising was there and definite swelling, but not nearly as bad as it could've been because he held back a bit on his punches. Her eye wasn't swollen shut and she absorbed most of the impact with the side of her head in effort to avoid his fist altogether.

"I'm sorry I hit you, Gigi," he said, looking into her eyes.

"I'm not, but I don't ever want you to do that again," she replied honestly.

"And I won't as long as your respect me and shit," he promised.

"I wanted to kill you in your sleep for putting your hands on me, you know."

"Damn, ma, I know you on go, but you ready to whack me behind that li'l shit?" Rob asked with a look of disgust on his face.

"All of my mom's boyfriends used to hit me and take advantage of me as a young girl growing up, and I've been through so many abortions and forced miscarriages that I've lost count, all because my mom needed her medicine - what I later found out to be heroin. I grew tired of the assaults and niggas threatening me and treating me like I was dirt on a public restroom floor, so I used my charms to convince my mother's landlord to let me come over to his house while my mom had company one night. That night changed my life because after he fell asleep from watching reruns of *Sanford and Son,* I searched until I found the pistol I always saw him with in the kitchen drawer. I used that same pistol and blew the next perverted mu'fucka that tried to touch me through the wall and threatened to take my mom's life if she ever ratted me out. I never took shit from nobody since."

Her story made Rob feel like shit for hitting her. Here he was looking at the hardened outer shell of her, and never did he imagine her to be so broken inside. He kissed her lips and wiped away her tears, then wrapped her up in his body. "You ain't gotta worry about that shit no more, ma. I got you, and you ain't leaving my side."

Gianna couldn't explain why, but she trusted his words. Rob was different, and she knew he could probably have any bitch he wanted, especially after acquiring his father's position in life. But he was choosing, and she knew that if she played her cards right, the two of them could go far. She'd heard the lines too many times before only to dip on the ones who were either too weak to handle her or too disloyal to stay true to their word. Something about Rob told her that he would be the real deal, and that made her feel safe and secure. He wasn't hardened by the streets nor was he a killer like her, but his thuggish ways were definitely his way of life and not just some façade like so many other niggas in the streets carried.

"I got somewhere for us to go tonight," Rob stated, thinking about his scheduled dinner with his mom.

"Is that so?" She looked into his eyes after feeling his muscle harden against her body.

"Yeah, but first I wanna handle a few things in between now and then." He smiled mischievously.

"And I'm sure I can think of a few too." She spoke her words between kisses on his lips while she began to massage him to full thickness.

"I see that you're a great mind reader."

Together they laughed before he scooped her up, and she immediately wrapped her thighs around his waist. After their tongues began to wrestle, she reached for him and stuffed the huge tip between her folds as he stepped underneath the waterfall shower and guided her up and down his entire length with her back flush against the tiled wall.

"Fuck me hard, Rob. I need that gangsta shit you got hiding inside of you to come out and handle this pussy good," she moaned as he stroked her harder and deeper.

Rob felt like his shit had grown another inch or two after hearing her talk like that.

"You ain't said shit, love." He bit down on her neck, squeezed her thick ass cheeks with both hands, and lifted her higher before dropping her down roughly on all of his inches.

"Faster baby, uhhh, ha-harder, oww shit, yeah!" Gianna screamed as he stretched her to the limit and a series of orgasms popped off, leaving his dick creamy as it sawed through and through.

"I ain't through with you," he stated as he felt her release before taking a seat on the bench in the shower with her still in his hands.

She then placed a foot on either side of his body on the bench and rode him hard until he dumped a heavy load off inside of her womb.

Chapter 9

Judge Utopi couldn't imagine his life being much better than it was now as he sat in the special hierarchy booth at Candy Ice, a gentlemen's club owned by the secret organization that had truly turned his life into a dream come true. He was commonly treated like royalty at the establishment, and the girls loved him because he was a big tipper who loved to have the ladies provide extra special services for his members-only big payouts.

"Having a nice day Judge?" Cherry, a high yellow-skinned stripper asked in the sexiest voice he'd ever heard before.

At age fifty-three, Judge Utopi was in the best shape of his life, and he thanked God that he was able to keep up with the young women walking around his earthly paradise. Sweat glistened on her forehead from the incredible heat around the place, making her edges stick to her skin like baby hairs. The look was enticing to the judge, who also loved the musky smell of a woman's pussy after a slight workout. He loved the natural scent of a woman, straight up.

"Not really having any luck with the ladies tonight, Cee," he lied, playing with the string on her skimpy thong.

"Is that right?" Cherry purred in his ear. She was so close to him she licked his neck and bit on his ear before crawling into his lap. "I have to ask though…" she added while rubbing her ass all over his crotch.

"Ask as you may, sweetness," he replied while reaching into his Burberry coat to reveal a wad of crispy hundreds.

"Do you love your sundaes with cherry on top?"

"Baby, you have no idea just how much I do," the judge said, then reached between them and removed his modest-sized penis.

"Oooh, is that for me?" Cherry licked her glossed lips and stared as he stroked himself.

"All of it," he said handing her the ten thousand dollars he knew he'd need to fuck her down, per policy.

"Tell you what," Cherry said, clutching the money in her left fist while reaching for his dick with her right. The swiftness in her motions would've never gone noticed, not even by the best of them, but the deafening wails escaping the judge's mouth couldn't be mistaken for anything other than a human in terror of losing his or her life. The pitch was so high no one would be able to distinguish its sex. "Mr. Mackmillions wanted you to know that your entire family died tonight before I put you outta your misery."

The strength which she used to slice open his throat nearly severed his head from his body. Nothing satisfied her more than righting the wrong done to such an important man in her life after all the years that were stolen from them. The sight before her was one she knew he'd enjoy, and after snapping several photos with her throwaway, she sent them to him with a kissing emoji before finishing her job. She sliced the judge's arms from his hands down to his elbow on both sides and watched the crimson-red blood leave his body in a hurry. Once that was done, she opened a hole in his throat and stuffed his severed penis inside, then sliced across his forehead, back and forth. The nerves in his body still reacted as he left this world for the next. Mere minutes passed before all the fun was over and his body lay limp against the back on his chair.

$$$$$

Mackmillions sat inside of his old school Chevy plotting with Max as his phone began to vibrate in his lap. After viewing the caller, he pressed the screen and slid it upwards to answer. The light immediately activated on Cherry's camera, illuminating the bloody scene she'd leave for the owners to clean.

"How are you feeling, love?" Mackmillions asked when her face came into view. He could never grow tired of seeing her angelic face.

"Just glad to be back on the job," Em stated.

"Did he pay you?" Mackmillions chuckled.

"Most definitely, and in more ways than one," she smiled.

"I know that got your juices flowing. And the list goes on," Mackmillions replied, returning her smile as Max fired up the supercharged engine.

"And so do we, until there's nothing left of them."

Max threw the car in drive and sped away from the parking lot of the private gentleman's club.

$$$$$

"Hi, I'm Jalamon, and it's nice to finally meet you in person and even more of a pleasure to have been in your presence."

Ambrea was taken aback by the well-dressed handsome Hispanic man before her. He took her hand and kissed the top of it, a gentle gesture. Young Mack smiled at the open show of affection coming from the Valdez family thus far. He suspected that they were a power family here in Mexico as were many others. He didn't know how far up the totem pole these guys were, but he would not be taking them lightly and that was for damn sure.

Miguel Valdez was the last to show, but show he did. Alongside him were two extremely beautiful and sexy Latina women, and one followed behind them. Each woman easily could have been a supermodel by American standards.

"Always the center of attention," Jalamon stated as his older half-brother stepped into his open arms.

"I could never steal a room from you, little brother." Miguel smiled handsomely in all of his glory.

"Yeah, but they could," Jalamon nodded to the Mexican beauties.

"And that's why they're here." They both laughed at that before Miguel's attention went elsewhere. "My baby sister is the world's most beautiful woman, don't you agree?" he asked the lovely triple threat he'd entered with.

"Sí papi," the women snickered together while admired the sight of Stephanie Valdez.

"Thank you, brother," Stephanie replied in her native tongue, loving the attention altogether and hoping that Young Mack looked at her the same way. She didn't even know him, yet felt a strong gravitational pull towards him.

"Ayyye, Ambrea!" Miguel crooned as he gracefully moved over and surprisingly embraced her.

"Ooohhh, hi to you too." Ambrea chuckled, intending to get beneath Stephanie's skin, but her attention was unfortunately elsewhere.

Young Mack held Stephanie's strong gaze as her brothers talked with Ambrea. He sensed that she wanted him, and she wasn't making it a secret from anyone how she felt either. As he stared into her beautiful honey hazels, the conspicuous looks she was giving him while biting into her bottom lip were starting to brick him up.

"The video guy" Miguel said, sizing Young Mack up.

"I'm Mack," Young Mack announced while extending his hand.

"Yeah, me too, see?" Miguel laughed and showcased his beauties. It was clear that he'd been drinking heavily before he arrived and safe to say that he'd been through a fine share of cocaine too. "So." He clapped his hands and all three women moved into the kitchen area at once. He then turned to Ambrea and spoke something in English, but mostly Spanish.

Young Mack couldn't understand all of the Spanish, but he caught on to some parts of it and never showed any emotions.

"Your goal will be to turn Gurdo's financials into Valdez financials," Miguel stated briefly and directly.

"We already have everything in place for the takeover and your involvement will be little to none and seem non-existent to the eyes of anyone outside this room," Jalamon added, trying to ensure her of her safety if she cooperated.

"If everything is as you say it is, then why do you need me?" Ambrea had serious reservations about going along with these people who were clearly out to harm her husband.

"Simply put, we need fingerprints, and you'll have no issues obtaining banking coordinates," Stephanie spoke up.

"This is my husband we're talking about here, and you want me to betray him, then live with myself while looking into his pain for however long we shall live after." Ambrea nervously looked into the eyes of everyone involved.

"Pity that you're not even faithful to the man you so much claim to love," Stephanie announced her distaste with Ambrea.

Ambrea shot daggers with her piercing stare at the heartless bitch that she hated so much already. Stephanie had no problem reminding her of the blemishes, and that shit got to her with ease. "No amount of dick can ever change my loyalty," Ambrea stated honestly. "Plus if I'm caught, he'll surely kill me."

"Chica, I'm sorry to tell you this, but you're not in a position to deny us," Miguel stated with a deadly gaze. It was the first time since he'd been there that she was able to see the darkness that was in his soul portals.

"Listen, Ambrea," Jalamon spoke, then sat down on the arm of the couch right next to her. "Give yourself the best shot at surviving this whole thing by giving us what we seek, and that way you know for sure that at least your family won't die over your bad decision making if you don't."

Ambrea knew that she was wrong for cheating, and she hated herself for it now. Young Mack could see the dilemma disastrously playing out in her mind but what didn't go unnoticed was that immediate danger they'd both be in if she made the wrong decision right here and now.

"Can I talk to her in private for a minute?" Young Mack requested and the Valdez family granted his request.

Stephanie was the last to leave with her eyes pressed into slits, daring him not to do what she thought he was about to do and console her. He smiled at the thought of how possessive this broad was, and he didn't even belong to her.

"Listen, Brea, I know shit is all over the place up top right now, but this war between them and Gurdo is above you and I. We mean absolutely nothing to these people, ma, and they could knock our cups over right now if they chose to. But on the other hand, think about Ash and your mother, because they certainly don't deserve to be caught up in any of this shit."

"And I do?" she cut him off.

"That's not what I'm implying, and you know it, so get ahold of yourself and know I'm rocking with you on whatever you decide here. I'm just tryna help you see through the murky water, because from where I'm sitting, it looks like you've allowed defeat to set in, and that's gonna get us both killed, and these people will go on fighting against Gurdo as if we never existed. Now our only shot to come out on top and give us both a fighting chance is to give them what they want and let them deal with Gurdo." He gave her a wink that only they could notice. "Don't let these people kill us on their turf, ma, because the videos will go out anyway and then Gurdo will be hunting us down himself if we did make it outta here alive."

"Damn," Ambrea exhaled, and tears flooded her eyes and created a silent river down her cheeks.

"I'm really nothing in this situation and they know it, so dead or alive they could give two shits about me. You're our only ticket outta here and possibly away from this entire situation."

"Okay, Mack, I'll do it," Ambrea stated, sniffling back the fluid that threatened to escape her nose.

"Be careful, and keep them convinced," Young Mack stated while waving the Valdezes over. They came and retook their seats around the living room and listened to everything Ambrea had to say about their enemy.

"If I do this, then you have to promise to take him out, because he won't allow me to live if he ever found out. This will be something I'll have to take to my grave or send him to his without knowing of it."

"We'll protect you," Jalamon promised.

"No, we won't," Stephanie countered her brother's last statement.

"Quiet!" Miguel yelled at his younger siblings before they could spark one of their famous arguments. "You help us with this we'll protect you and your family and make sure that neither of you want for anything so as long as you shall live."

"I already said I'll do it, so let's stop talking about it. Just don't make me regret it because death is always more alluring than betrayal."

"We won't let you down," both brothers answered in unison.

$ $ $ $ $

"Tell me my eyes are playing tricks on me," Gurdo said as his heart threatened to shatter into a million pieces once he laid eyes on his wife walking outside of his enemy's mansion and getting into a waiting black SUV.

"What the hell is she doing there? Oh shit, look!" Daniel, Gurdo's right-hand man, stated after watching Young Mack leave the mansion behind Ambrea and get into the back of the same SUV as if Gurdo wasn't seeing it for himself. "Should we intercept them at the airport?" Daniel wanted to stain his hands with their blood.

"And which one would that be, genius? This is Houston and there are too many to pinpoint their exact landing location," Gurdo replied.

"You're right. I just can't believe this shit," Daniel stated in his native tongue after becoming so heated.

"She's never given me reason to doubt her loyalty," Gurdo said to himself as he controlled the stealth drone that had successfully flown over his enemy's fence line the first of many trials. Many other attempts had been made but to no avail. Their house was a fortress and was protected by military grade security systems. Gurdo's trigger finger began to itch and murder raged in his mind, but his heart was heavy, and he desperately needed some answers and quick.

"Give me six of these and every weapon in this warehouse," Gurdo demanded to his new arms dealer.

"Showtime, fellas. Load this shit up!" Daniel yelled in Spanish to their workers.

"Your payment will be wired within an hour," Gurdo shook hands with the dealer before leaving the warehouse with Daniel on his heels. Gurdo's mind was heavy, and Daniel could see the deep worry lines that creased his forehead as they slid into the back of Gurdo's awaiting Rolls Royce Phantom.

"What's up, brother?" Daniel asked, truly concerned about his boss and best friend since grade school.

"I know her. She would never betray me or my family like that. The level we're on is way beyond her level of understanding and shit can spiral out in the blink of an eye."

"So what are you saying?" Daniel asked.

"Something is wrong and I need to get to the bottom of it."

"It didn't look like she was being forced to do anything. And how do you explain the backstabbing vato being there with her?" Daniel wasn't about to play the fool and wind up dead and stinking somewhere. He was going at Young Mack no matter what his best friend and boss decided to do with his bitch. The way he saw it, he could always find ways to make her disappear if need be.

"That's the part I can't wrap my mind around."

"Yeah, well, just don't let it make you out to be a fool. The family is counting on us to hold it down and I'm at your hip at all times, brother," Daniel assured.

"Likewise."

$ $ $ $ $

"KenKen, why am I not surprised to see you here?" Rob asked with a chip on his shoulder.

"I come in peace, brother man." KenKen smiled, knowing he was not a threat to Rob unless it was warranted. "Need to talk to you for a quick second, if that's cool with you."

"Wait for me in the car, ma," Rob ordered Gianna, who did as was requested.

KenKen took in the opportunity to take in all of Gigi's sexy body in her form-fitting Givenchy dress with the mesh sidings. He could see her bare hips and knew there was nothing underneath her dress. Rob noticed his eyes following closely with Gigi's every step. He didn't say anything, but he did make a mental note to question Gianna about their relationship, if there was one to question.

"What's on yo' mind, bruh?" Rob asked as he slid into the backseat next to KenKen in his Rover.

"Just wanted to see how you felt about The Realm so far."

"There's nothing to feel something about. Hell, I don't know shit about it, and to be perfectly honest, I don't even think I wanna know shit about it." Rob really didn't give a shit what any of them thought about how he felt. He didn't know anything about this so-called Realm or its members.

"So, I guess it's safe to say that you wouldn't be interested in chasing a better position then?" KenKen desperately wanted to know.

"KenKen, brother, I'm already in the streets, and the way I feel is like this ... mufuckas is already threatening to bring harm to me and my mother for some hush hush shit we know nothing about, then forcing me into a business I know nothing about, so it's safe to say that these Realm mu'fuckas don't give a shit about none of y'all. Me, I'm a jackboy by trade and by heart, and all this running businesses and shit is taking away from that. If I gotta play, then this shit gotta pay," Rob expressed himself truthfully, and those were the words KenKen needed to hear.

"Don't sweat shit, young homie. You just ride and I'll gas this bitch. But you gotta be ready for anything at any time dealing with these people. They have a lot of reach and a lot of power, and when you add their money, anything they want to happen can and probably will happen."

"Ready for anything like what?"

"I wanna take this shit over from the inside out," KenKen confessed.

"The Realm?"

"Just ride, li'l homie, we got this," KenKen stated before jumping on his phone.

Rob took that as his cue to step out, so he slid from the confines of KenKen's Rover and waved Gigi over.

Damn, she do be killing shit, he thought to himself as she sashayed her way over to him.

"What?" she gushed from the way he was looking at her.

"Damn near wanna eat you up and say the hell with dinner." They laughed, but knew he meant every word.

"Can't let you knock me outta meeting your mom just because you horny as hell, like always," Gianna stated, then rang his mother's doorbell.

"What'chu doing? She gon' think we the neighbors or some shit!" Rob laughed and used his keys to unlock the door just as his mother turned the knob to open it.

"Oooh, wow, you really brought company," Mary said with a warming smile.

"Wanted us to surprise you," Rob smiled, then made the introductions.

"Well, y'all come on in here. Dinner is just about ready." Mary waved them in, leaving the door open for them, and headed into the kitchen to remove her famous pot roast from the slow cooking oven.

"I wanted to do something fancy for us tonight, but decided against it and made your dad's favorite meal. I'm glad I did, because there will be plenty."

"Cool, because we're starving." Rob winked at Gigi.

"That's why that girl so skinny over there, but I'ma fatten her right on up."

"Skinny?" Rob asked. "She thick as Megan, Ma."

"Megan? Now who in the world is Megan?" Mary asked, clueless as to who they were referring to.

"Thee Stallion, Ma."

"She's a really big rapper, and he ain't talking about nothin'," Gigi stated.

"Is she the one with that real big booty that be making all those funny noises?" Mary asked.

"Nawl, that's Cardi, Ma. Have you been sleeping under a rock or something?" Rob laughed.

"Now who in the hell is Cardi?" Mary asked dumbfoundedly.

Her question sent Rob and Gianna into a convulsion of laughter. Her lack of knowledge in the hip hop culture of the new was humorous.

"Just too many personalities for me," Mary added.

"We can see that," Rob chuckled.

"So a mother must ask," Mary began, "are you two a couple?"

Gianna eyed Rob, gauging his reaction while surprisingly feeling nervous at the same time.

"What you looking at me like that for?" Rob laughed from her apparent suspense.

"Boy, stop playing with that woman's emotions. You know why she's looking to you for an answer, and now you got us both in limbo!" his mother stated before playfully hitting him in his arm with her handkerchief.

"Ah, okay!" He laughed while enjoying his time with them. "Yeah, Ma, that's my boo right there, and I can't even lie if I wanted to because I'm feeling her something serious. I just don't want us to rush into it. I want us to grow into it."

Gianna lowered her face, but her smile was apparent as it stretched her entire face, and the tears that misted her eyes were threating to erupt at any second. She'd never felt accepted since her birth parents passed away, and after years of being in foster care growing up, it made it clear that everyone was out for self.

They talked and ate into the wee hours of the night before Rob and Gianna made their exit.

"You do know I'm fucking you to sleep tonight, right?" he spoke into her ear as he hugged her with her back to him.

"You ain't really saying shit," Gianna sexily teased him, grinding her ass against his crotch before turning around in his arms while putting her back to the passenger door of his ride.

"You know I been killing it though, so stop flexing."

"Flex for what? I'm officially Mrs. Rob now. I got the juice, babe," Gigi bragged while giving his growing organ a slight squeeze.

"Oh, so you're up now." The sound of a revving engine interrupted their moment and grabbed both of their attention.

Rob ice grilled the occupants of the tinted vehicle and put himself in front of his woman. Gigi took the hint and smoothly took both weapons from the small of his back without the opposition or whoever it was in the car being able to see her movements. Gianna then stepped before her man and raised both weapons in the directions of the revving vehicle, ready to make Swiss cheese outta them. The driver quickly reversed the car and got out of sight down the block and into the night.

"Fuck was that?" Rob's adrenaline was high as he opened the door for her to climb inside the cabin of his Bentley, the car he had inherited form his father's collection.

"No sweat, baby. I already know who they are and they were just making sure that I knew they know too," Gianna said as she seated herself behind the wheel. "That was Tony's baby mother's brother."

"Oh, word?"

"Spanish cats with a lot of heart and a helluva lot of go."

"Fuck they doing showing up here outta all places? That's going to be a major problem."

"Damn straight it is," Gigi agreed with her mind already made up. She knew there was no way to allow the slight to pass, especially now that she knew they knew the murder was on her hands. People like them never knocked, but they gave her the chance to know they were coming, and she would make it their worst mistake.

$ $ $ $ $

Agent Chandler and his partner Agent Drexler stood perplexed as they looked over the murder scene at Club Candy Ice. Forensics crowded the area, combing through everything to find anything that would ultimately lead to the perpetrator of this heinous crime.

"A federal magistrate dead in the private section of a strip joint," Drexler stated, finding it sorta amusing.

"Mu'fucka gotta have some nuts to pull this one off," Chandler replied.

"Or some fire-ass pussy." Drexler chuckled at the irony of his joke.

The perpetrator was deemed gruesomely sadistic in the murder of Judge Utopi, cutting his throat and shoving his penis into the gaping incision and burning his body with hydrochloric acid to top it all off. It was definitely an overkill, and Chander read it as a message to something much greater than the murder of a federal judge.

"You's a real dick sometimes, Drex," Chandler stated while walking away from the horrible scene.

As they stepped out into the club's main area, the boys in blue were everywhere, interviewing witnesses and searching patrons. He nearly made it out the front entrance before being stopped by a gorgeous, long-nailed blonde dancer with wide hips, and he could tell she had a fatty behind her from the way she walked.

"Hey Detective!" she summoned his attention.

Chandler stopped and took in everything about her and he couldn't help but to stare at her camel toe.

"What's poppin', ma?"

"Oh, word? So what are you supposed to be, a gangsta or some shit?" she asked, finding his act a bit corny.

"I was born in the boogey down and raised out in Jersey, but you don't know what that'll do to a young boy heading into adulthood."

"Shiiit, don't look like it did nothing wrong to you now you all FBI agent and shit." She smiled, admiring that he wasn't putting on to impress her and that he was actually from the streets for real.

"What can I do for you?" he asked, ready to get down to the reason she stopped him and get back to work.

"What if I knew someone that knew something about the murder here tonight?"

"Call 222-TIPS, ma. You know how that shit go."

"No, actually I don't, because I ain't no damn snitch. But being that you're all cute and shit and I like your flavor, I'd be willing to disclose this witness's name and number for you over dinner and some hard sex."

"Damn." Chandler exhaled, feeling his shit knot up. "I didn't get your name, ma."

"Oh, I'm Porshea, but everyone calls me Cherry."

"Most def then. Here's my card, and I'm Agent Chandler."

"And I'm Agent Drexler, baby girl," his partner chimed in, stepping next to him.

"Hi," Cherry smiled at the chubby agent that looked too much like Cedrick the Entertainer.

"Hey," Drexler stated with a smile and a wink.

Agent Chandler walked away from his irritating partner yet again and made his way outside into the night's cool breeze.

"Nice night," Drexler said, leaning back against the hood of their work car.

"Sure is, but something is definitely going on. I have a hunch it's gonna be some major shit, and this is just the beginning."

Chapter 10

Ambrea exhaled a long breath after entering the confines of her home. It had been one helluva day dealing with those lunatic muthafuckers who called themselves the Valdezes. The plane ride back to Houston from Mexico was uneventful between her and Young Mack with them having so much on their minds individually, plus he stayed glued to his phone the entire time. She kicked off her red bottoms and fell flat on her back in the California king-sized bed she shared with her kingpin husband and sometimes their pit bull. Tired wasn't the word to fit her extreme fatigue, especially without being able to sleep on the plane. Her relaxation period didn't last as long as it took to close her eyes because she was sure she had heard something in there with her.

The scratchy strike of her husband's favorite Zippo lighter sounded before the yellowish-orange flame lit up his indignant face and the tip of what she knew to be his favorite coconut hash-flavored kush.

"Why are you sitting here in the dark, my love?" Ambrea spoke in Spanish before turning on the lamp from the nightstand.

Strangely, after illuminating the room, she couldn't see his face, but only saw a figure standing next to her man. She guessed due to the shine glistening from the customized chrome handgun in the standing figure's hand that it was Daniel, her man's right hand.

"Gurdo, what's he doing in our bedroom?" she asked as calmly as her nervous self could muster.

"Where have you been, Ambrea?" Gurdo asked with a level voice.

"Out handling some business, like I told you I would be."

"Business like what?" He was getting heated just thinking about her betraying him.

"My own private business, which I don't wanna talk about in front of your friend."

"Oh, you don't have much of a choice in the matter, chica," Daniel spoke up.

"My name is Ambrea, Daniel, and if you ever address me as anything other than that again, it'll be a race to see who'll get a dirt nap first!" she stated while removing the .40 cal from underneath her pillow that she always slept with.

"B——" Daniel started but was quickly interrupted.

"Calm down, brother," Gurdo ordered in Spanish with the back of his hand against Daniel's chest.

"So, you'll shoot one of our own now?" Gurdo asked accusingly.

"I will not ask you to make anyone respect me, Gurdo. I'm from the streets too, even though I don't carry myself that way, and I demand my respect."

"Respect?" Gurdo yelled, slamming his glass of Hennessey up against the wall, spilling its contents everywhere.

The sudden burst of anger frightened her and she nearly let off a shot in his direction just form reflex.

"You speak of respect at a time like this?" Gurdo couldn't control the tears that escaped his red eyes and wet his face.

"What are you talking about?" Ambrea was truly clueless.

"You betray me with the enemy and you act as if you know nothing. That's very disrespectful," Gurdo stood and reached into the small of his back and removed the Llama .45 and held it at his side.

"You need to calm down. It is not what you're thinking." Ambrea's voice shook as she realized the seriousness of the situation before her.

"I loved you with all my heart." Gurdo let the anguish and the tears out of captivity.

"You love me. Gurdo, don't use past tense with me because I would never betray you in the way that you're accusing me of."

Gurdo wiped his face, already tired of the tears wetting his face. "Had I not spotted you coming from their home with my own two eyes…"

"Can you allow me a chance to clear this up? To clear your thoughts. And after I explain myself, whatever decision you make, I'll accept it as what it is," Ambrea stated and tossed the weapon off the bed.

Gurdo and Daniel watched as the weapon hit the floor before their feet.

"All honesty, no matter the hurt," she stated, ready to confess to her true reason for being in the enemy's presence.

Gurdo's sat himself down and rested his weapon on his knee without removing his finger from the trigger guard.

"Your enemies, the Valdezes, infiltrated the rented villa we used while in Mexico. You know I know nothing of who your enemies are with the mediocre role I have in your business, but on our last day there - you know, the evening you woke me with your tongue…" Ambrea smiled at the memory but quickly continued. "Before you returned, well, a cleaning lady walked into the bathroom on me as I was stepping out of the shower and frightened the hell outta me. She moved as if I had scared her as well, but I absentmindedly asked her not to leave but to continue doing her job as I knew we were leaving that day. She apologized as I wrapped myself in a towel - the same one you found me sleeping in. "Well, I moved to the bed and immediately fell asleep, but I forgot my phone in the shower. I-I was using it t-to watch videos of myself with someone else." She paused as tears came rushing out. She could see the flexing of his jawline and knew he was beyond angry, but she promised to tell the truth, and that's exactly what she was gonna do no matter the hurt feelings. "When you woke me, I was shaken because I remembered the phone still being there and I didn't want you to find it but while you were pleasing me. I looked over and saw the phone on the nightstand and thought maybe I did bring it out with me. Anyways, that cleaning woman had put it there with a note to hit her up, or she'd be sure to send you the videos. So, I contacted her, ready to pay anything not to have those videos released to you and assuming that the woman was a poor cleaning lady living in Mexico. But it turns out that the cleaning woman wasn't poor, nor was she a cleaning woman at all."

Gurdo clenched his fist tight as he and Daniel listened intently.

"It was Stephanie Valdez the entire time, and when I made it to the address given to me, I knew in my gut that something was wrong. After being escorted by armed men to the back of her home, she introduced herself and explained that she had come to the villa to kill you, but you weren't there, and after searching my phone, she decided to let me live, only to try and manipulate me into transferring your wealth over to them to cripple the family."

Daniel looked at his right-hand man and saw the fury in his eyes and knew he believed her lying ass.

"You rocking with this shit, homie?" he asked, but got no reply in return.

"There's nothing to it, Daniel. It was either I agree to do the shit, or sacrifice my love for him and die either way. Surely he would not forgive me if the truth about me sleeping with someone else came from anywhere other than me."

"You should kill yourself, if you asked me," Daniel spit.

"I'm glad we're not asking you shit stupid! The only way for me to leave that place alive was to agree to the deal or else he would've gotten the videos and my dead body. What don't you get about that!"

"How do you explain Young Mack being there?" Daniel grilled her, still feeling she'd made the story up.

Ambrea dropped her head and the tears started again because she knew her truth was killing her husband slowly. "It was him in the videos, and he was there to support me in the purchase," she confessed.

"His bitch ass is dead! Gee, let me send a team at him, snake muthafucka!" Daniel fumed.

Gurdo had yet to say anything, but his anger was visible in every way. "How long were you gonna wait to tell me this?" Gurdo finally spoke with blood-stained red eyes.

"I was planning to tell you everything about my affair before anything and depending on your reaction to that, I had it set in my mind to gather my family and disappear. I don't want your money, Gurdo, and I definitely want no parts in some drug war where I'm in the center of both sides' crosshairs."

"So you weren't planning to hand us over to those coyotes?" Gurdo believed his woman was being sincere because she had never given him reason to doubt her ever.

"I'm home, aren't I? I know I fucked up. The thing with Young Mack has been going on before our time, and I made him promise not to fall in love with me. He's never pursued me, Gurdo. I wouldn't lie about that. It's always been me because you're never around and he knows me in ways no one ever has. No excuses, but I can prove to you that they lured me there and tried to force me into betraying you."

"Show me the proof," Gurdo stated almost too quick for Daniel's taste. If it was him, he'd kill her, Young Mack, and the Valdez's bitch asses.

Ambrea moved until she stood before her husband before lowering to her knees while never losing eye contact with him.

"Yo, what the fuck you on?" Daniel protested.

"Nigga, you in my shit so you can always get the fuck out!" Ambrea hissed, looking him over like he was crazy.

She proceeded to pull out her phone and send the message crushing the Valdez's plans to use her as their pawn. Once it was sent, she handed Gurdo her phone for him to read the response.

"She's gonna send you the videos we went there to destroy, but promise me you won't look at them. I am madly in love with you and I seriously love being wifey. Promise me," she pleaded, but got no reply.

The wait wasn't long at all. When the reply came back, it was nothing sweet and everything sour. Stephanie Valdez sent threat after threat to her inbox without rest. Gurdo had his proof that his woman was being truthful, and his fury with his enemies powered his forgiveness for her misdeeds, but he was ready for blood to stain his hands.

"Ready the attack drones, Daniel. These roaches gotta die!" Gurdo fumed before his personal phone began to vibrate. His business line soon followed, and so did Daniel's.

Ambrea squeezed his hand with desperate, pleading eyes. She had proven herself honest, and now she needed her husband to show her he was still with her and not look at those videos.

"Please," she mouthed without sound.

"Just you and him?" Gurdo asked.

"I swear on my soul," she replied with tears cascading her pretty face.

"Daniel, give me your phone," Gurdo ordered.

"Wh-what for?"

"Give me your damn phone and I won't ask again!" Gurdo growled without looking in his direction.

Daniel handed both of his phones to Gurdo, who then gave them all to Ambrea and used his thumbs to wipe the tears from her wet face.

"You know what to do. I'm pretty sure those dumbasses haven't pinpointed our location just yet because they're too emotional so hurry before they do," Gurdo stated with one final pull from his blunt, ready to get his hands dirty.

"What about the backstabber, homie?" Daniel pressed after Ambrea left them.

"Send a wet team, fuck you mean?" Gurdo looked at his best friend and brother from another like he must've forgotten his deadly get down.

$ $ $ $ $

"Ma! Where y'all at?" Young Mack yelled once he was finally safe inside the comfort of his parents' mini mansion.

"We're in here, boy, stop all that noise!" Sylvia yelled back.

Young Mack walked into the living room and saw that his mom and Aeriella were deeply engrossed in a game of Scrabble. The sight brought him solace after such an edgy situation.

"Hello stranger." Aeriella smiled after he failed to speak to them.

"Where are all those manners your mother and father instilled in you?" Sylvia asked, speaking of herself in third person.

"What's poppin', ladies?" he spoke with a generous smile.

"Ain't nothing up. She kickin' me in my money maker," Sylvia stated, and they all laughed.

"Ma, where's Pop?"

"Out making funeral homes rich, acting like I don't know how him and Max get down, especially after putting me to sleep. Boy, I swear that man was blessed by Allah up above!" Sylvia laughed at the disgusted faces of her son and future daughter-in-law.

"Come on, Ma!" Young Mack whined.

"Boy, y'all act like we eighty years old or some shit. Yeah, we get busy, and ya pop be fucking my hips outta place. Been

132

getting steroid shots in both hips since before yo' ass was born!"

"I'm outta here, Ma, you wildin'!" Young Mack laughed hard before calling out to Aeriella.

"Good, call yo' damn attack dog, 'cause her ass wasn't even gon' let me win one anyway," Sylvia went on.

"Love you, Ma!" Young Mack yelled over his shoulder as he and Aeriella made their way upstairs.

Once inside his room, he wrapped her up in his strong arms. His experience with the Valdez family was the closest he'd been to certain extinction, unarmed and unable to protect himself.

"What's all this, Mackentosh Miller?" Aeriella asked in a warm, caring voice. He loved the way she felt being wrapped up in his arms.

"I just miss you, that's all."

"You talking like you've been gone for days," she giggled.

He moved her body back a step before staring into her eyes for an intense minute.

"Can I kiss you? Like you used to let me do when we were younger." His question caught her a bit off guard.

"What's the matter, Mack? You're acting weird for some odd reason."

"Because I wanna kiss you? What's weird about that? Because it's the least I wish to do to you." He smiled.

"Yes, you can kiss me, Mackentosh Miller." Aeriella smiled because she knew he would only let her and two other people in his life call him by his government name and get away with it.

He didn't hesitate one bit to wrap her back up in his arms while caressing her ample butt with both his hands. He pulled her body close and stared into her eyes once again.

"Extra," she chuckled before their lips found one another's.

He loosened his grip on her butt and began rubbing all over it while attempting to invade her mouth with his tongue. She was getting extremely turned on by his carefulness with her and she allowed her walls to come down the more he advanced. Young Mack knew that he loved her and had never stopped even in her absence from his life, and now that she was back, he wanted all of her and he was destined to get it. He wanted to make love to her and reclaim her heart as his own, if only she would just trust him with her. His lips moved from her mouth and slowly down to her neck, where he remembered all too well where her spot had been when they were teenagers.

"Mack…sss," she wheezed, feeling her juices drench her panties.

"Why are you fighting me? Can't you see that I need you?" he asked sincerely.

"Because you're gonna hurt me," she replied while sucking in her breath after feeling the hardness of his erection press against her midriff.

"I just don't get it." He released her body and they stood there silently.

"You're mad, right?" Aeriella asked, feeling flushed from embarrassment, plus she was horny as hell at the same time.

"Nah, I'm straight," he lied without looking her in the eyes.

"You're lying, I can tell," she said, then turned to leave.

He couldn't let her go again after all those years of missing her. He rushed to catch up to her and grabbed her before she could open his room door.

"Mack," she gasped as he held her around her slim waist and sucked her neck hard like she used to do him as kids.

"I ain't giving up. Now you got a hater mark for all them niggas that be shooting. They'll know you're taken." He laughed as she rushed to the bathroom to see the passion mark.

"Why'd you do that?" she asked, amused by his antics. It had been some time now since she'd had any attention from any man like what Young Mack gave her so effortlessly.

"You belong to me, Aeriella, and the sooner you realize I just wanna love you and make you happy, the better it would be for the both of us, not to mention for all the li'l niggas I'd snuff out behind looking at you a certain way without me by your side."

"You're on it like that?" she asked, biting her bottom lip because he was still turning her on in a major way.

"And some, so you better get the arguments together now, because I'm punishing any nigga that step your way." The look in his eyes told her a story his actions wouldn't have to because she knew and always heard about his actions in the streets.

"Come here." She waved him over with her index finger.

He could clearly see the desire in her eyes. He'd always seen it; she just never opened up for him.

"Kiss me again," she ordered while taking his hand and putting it inside the waistband of her shorts and panties so that he could feel how wet and puffy he was making her.

"That's all me from now on, you hear me?" he stated as he began to undress her.

"You better not hurt me, Mackentosh Miller," she demanded.

"Hurt you? I'm about to make you Mrs. Miller, ma, now respect my gee and give me what's rightfully mine," he ordered as he hurried out of his own clothes and pressed his hardness at her opening.

"Ssss...condom, Mack." she lost her breath as he pushed only the head of his thickness inside of her.

"You really don't get it, do you?" he asked as he slowly eased himself in until only an inch or two could no longer fit.

"Sssshiiiit!" She gripped his body, pulling him close, and kissed his lips.

"I'm not letting you get away from me again, ma. I love you, always have," he confessed.

"Uhhh, I love you too, Mack, I swear I do."

"Then tell me not to pull out in the end and make me believe you," he said as he long-stroked her at a tortoise pace, torturing her burning desire for him to really sex her down.

"Please don't hurt me, Young Mack." A tear escaped her beautiful eyes as she stared him in the eyes.

"Marry me then."

She stopped his movements by pushing both hands against his chest while looking at him in shock. She could tell he was serious, but was he like really serious - like right now serious, she thought to herself.

"I won't be complete in this life or the next without you, A," he spoke sincerely as he began to slowly move in and out of her wetness again. He couldn't believe how wet she was.

"I love you, Mackentosh. Uhhh, shiiit you hitting my spot, ahhh!" Her orgasm rocked her with wave after wave of phenomenal exotic feelings.

"That's a yes?" He smiled at her sweet torture.

"Yes, yes, I'll be your wife!" she screamed, still tingling from the burst of orgasmic sensations.

"Fuck yeah!" he yelled. He kissed her hard at first, then lightened up as he began to make sweet love to her.

Chapter 11

"Aaaahhh! We should have killed that bitch!" Stephanie yelled, throwing one of her designer vases against the floor, shattering the ten-thousand-dollar piece of art.

She sat down on her leather sofa and put her face in her hands. She literally felt defeated as the thought of taking over Gurdo's assets and territories was drifting off in the distance.

"Calm down, love, all is not lost yet."

Stephanie looked up to her brothers as if they were a two-headed dragon as they busied themselves with some type of electronic devices.

"Do either of you care to enlighten me on what you two obviously know that you have yet to tell me about?"

"We're tracking the lover boy and have a team en route as we speak to extract him once they're in place," Jalamon stated without taking his eyes from the device.

A spark of hope invigorated her body, mind, and spirit as she had never thought to do that, even though she had his personal cell phone number. Just the thought of him and what he could do to her body sent tingling sensations through her clitoris and chilled her outer shell. The sensations made her moist between her folds and caused her thong panties to cling to her womanhood.

"What are we still doing here?" she asked surprisingly louder than she intended to.

"Don't worry, they'll bring him back alive, hopefully," Miguel proclaimed.

"I need to get there now!" Stephanie demanded with an outstretched hand.

Both of her brothers looked to each other before looking into her demanding gaze. The fire in her eyes told a tale they were way too familiar with. Miguel handed her the tracking screen and Jalamon elbowed him in his side.

"What?" he asked with that "you already know how she is" look.

Jalamon just shook his head at his older brother as they watched their only sister march away with authority.

$ $ $ $ $

"Mack, me tink me teke care oh dee nosey agent," Max said as he finished tying their latest victim to a chair in her home.

"In due time, Max, but for now, let's focus on Ms. Berry and the part she played in my demise."

Their victim struggled and mumbled incoherently as she recognized her dire situation. She'd recently awakened, and her memory came rushing back to her as she fought desperately to loosen the binds, but to no avail. The memory of walking from the grocery store with bags filling her hands and something being placed over her nose and mouth from behind came rushing back to her and piss escaped her bladder and wet her stretch pants and the seat beneath her.

"Looks like she has something to say, Max," Mackmillions patronized her before snatching the tape from over her mouth and causing her to groan out in pain.

"Mackentosh Miller, why are you doing this to me when you know I've always been on your side ever since we were kids in grade school?"

"Don't be so formal, Deb. You'll make my heart heavy after I'm done with you," Mackmillions reached his hand out

138

without taking his piercing eyes off of his prey. "I want names and roles, Deb. It's the only way for me to walk outta here without taking your life for the one they took away from me by locking me away from my family," Mackmillions said as Max opened the bag of weapons then handed it to him. Inside the bag was an assortment of surgical tools that made him smile at his trusted right hand. Max shrugged his shoulders with a grin that said "you're welcome".

"Please, Mack, it's not me you want, and you know it deep in your heart."

"Last chance to give me what I want," Mackmillions said, observing the long-handled scalpel for everyone to see.

Debrah shivered and vomit threatened to erupt from the depths of her stomach and through her mouth from the pain she knew would come to her from that weapon if he didn't change his mind about killing her. She really had nothing to give that he didn't already know.

"If it's gonna be back to the box with me, Deb, then I'm gonna make sure that it's to a different kind of box for everyone involved," Mackmillions stated, raising the scalpel high above her shaking kneecap.

"Deb! Babe, where are you?" a deep male's voice roared from the living room where the front door was located.

Mackmillions placed his index finger to his lips in hopes to quiet her whimpers. He threw his head towards the direction the voice came from, signaling Max to get active. Moments later, Max came pushing the dude through the door of the kitchen. The guy nearly stumbled from the force of Max shoving him.

"Wow, I never expected this," Mackmillions stated truthfully.

"Damn," the man sighed after realizing who'd taken over his home.

"Damned it is. Ken, it's been a minute, wouldn't you say?"

"Yeah, long time no see, Mack," KenKen stated hoarsely.

"Death has finally come knocking on your front door, but the question is, do you think you're man enough to answer it, or do you think you can outrun it?"

"Depends on the cause?" KenKen replied honestly.

"Who took me down?"

"The Realm did all of that, Mack. Jackson couldn't wait to get at you for killing his brother, that real estate guy. Now he's hell bent on taking the city away from the players."

Mackmillions sat perplexed by this news. There was no way that Jackson could have found out about the murder that fast without help of someone he trusted.

"Ba——" Debrah started, but was cut short.

"No! I gotta tell him what everyone has been scared to," KenKen stated before giving Mackmillions his undivided attention.

The things KenKen revealed to him were never apparent to him, but now things were starting to make much more sense than before. It explained why no one came to his aid in all these years. The order to banish him would certainly not be disobeyed by members of the Realm because it would be punishable by death to members and their families.

"Let me get this straight. You want me to trust you to go to war with me against my enemies, which included you for so many years?" Mackmillions chuckled at the thought of how much times had changed.

"I'm not the enemy, Mack, and we've never really had beef in this lifetime. I'm neutral in the whole of this situation and I have been under the umbrella of these egotistical fuck heads for too long now."

"The Realm!" Mackmillions chuckled, thinking of the organization.

"The new Realm. It wasn't always this bad, ya feel me? Once upon a time we were all able to eat out here. Now it's like the heads up above are straight vacuums for every fucking thing we risk our lives out here for," KenKen vented.

"I don't know, Ken, you could be working some type of angle or sum'n," Mackmillions stated nonchalantly while carefully cleaning under his finger nails with a shorter scalpel than the first.

"The only angle is to remove myself from the order of The Realm and keep safe the ones I hold dear to my heart."

Debrah wanted badly to hold on to her life's love with the fear of the unknown lying in wait.

"Deb, can I trust this man you love?" Mackmillions asked with death in his dark eyes.

Debrah looked over her man and studied his demeanor carefully. Sure as anything, she knew that she'd trust him with her life, but if he was working an angle and planning to renege, she wasn't sure and it caused her to have to study him. Confident in her man's stance and with the trust she held deep in her heart for him, she nodded her head in affirmation.

"That's nice, because it's gonna cost you your life if I even feel like he's on his bullshit." Mackmillions dropped the surgical tool back inside the bag Max had given him. He stood and removed his .45 S&W from his hip and pointed it at a flinching KenKen.

"Max, take her to the car, but leave her tied in case she gets any thoughts."

Max did as he was ordered.

"Call your driver and tell him to stand down." Mackmillions knew all too well how KenKen was groomed by Phatts and moved just as his mentor did.

KenKen slowly removed his phone and told his man to stand down as Max moved out of there carrying Debrah.

"Love you," he stated as mist formed in his eyes.

"Take care of your business and make it back to me," Debrah stated as tears wet her face while her heart rate increased form all the possibilities of the unknown up ahead.

"One hunnit. You know I got you," KenKen spoke in confidence.

"Now that that's outta the way, let's hear what you bring to the table." Mackmillions lowered his weapon and took a seat.

"Names, stash houses, rats, and most important to your cause over all the others, the director of the Bureau and his right hand."

"So they brought them in after all?" Mackmillions questioned aloud, but more to himself.

"What was that?"

"Ah, nothing, just thinking aloud."

Everything was starting to make sense now. His fall was definitely a plot for those greedy mu'fuckas he'd fed for years to take over something he'd created all on his own.

$ $ $ $ $

Rob stirred awake from the loud barking of his neighbor's pitbulls. He'd never heard them act up at this time of the morning. It was three in the morning and sleep was acting like a bitch that he'd once cheated on with her sister. He tossed the comforter off his body and swung himself into a sitting position. Looking back over his shoulder, he saw that sleep's sister must have been Gianna because she was out like a light - or so he thought. Slowly making his way downstairs, Rob looked towards the living room and saw that Pop and Monsta were both active in a game of NBA2K. The headsets they wore muted the TV's sound, making it easy for him to sneak up from behind them.

"Ahhh!"

"The fuck?"

Rob had slapped both of them behind their heads and quickly got their attention. "Fuck am I paying you two mu'fuckas to sit around and play games while there is clearly something going on outside?" Rob irritably stated before making his way in the opposite direction towards the dark kitchen.

"Get down!" Pop yelled, noticing the laser red beam chasing his mentor's movements.

It was the last thing Rob heard before thunderous shots rang out, awakening the night all around them. Debris of glass and wall particles showered Rob as he scrambled to get away from the threat of death.

Pop was unsure of the attackers situated outside, but the loud blasts from his automatic pump blew chunks from the inside of the home through the exterior as he continued to finger the trigger in retaliation.

Monsta stood from behind the couch and raised MP5s in both hands and started dumping in the same direction the shots were entering the house from while easing himself beside his brother to provide Rob plenty of cover. Rob hurriedly took the stairs in flight to his room to check on Gianna, who was no longer in bed where he'd left her. He felt a breeze and noticed that one of the windows was open, and the curtain floated in the air as the morning wind blew in.

"Fuck!" he growled to himself, hoping that she hadn't been taken.

He quickly moved to his closet, threw on a vest, and grabbed two .40s with twenty-two round extenders. He grabbed two extra clips after jamming the first one's home and finger fucked the action, snapping the fully automatic handguns into place. Looking outside of his bedroom window, he measured the distance before taking the leap and landing on top of the city's trash can, which caved in from the velocity of his weight crashing down on it. He quickly recovered and caught a knee while activating the beams on his weapons as he searched the darkness for any signs of the enemy approaching. Shots continued to ring out as he rounded the side of his home, headed towards the front in hopes of catching the enemy off guard. He spotted a Mexican cat squatting behind the front bumper of an old model Chevy Suburban while reloading a clip into a Draco pistol. Before he could complete his stand, Rob rocked that baby with a three-round burst from one of his .40s. The Mexican dropped on impact and struggled to raise his weapon in Rob's direction, but another burst of hollows opened his face like a pumpkin.

Two heavily-tatted Mexican cats rounded the Suburban and sent fire in Rob's direction. Rob dropped to the ground and let both of his weapons spit fire back at the aggressive attackers. Bullets found a home in both their bodies, but it only slowed them down, indicating that they were both real animals thirsty for the blood of him and his crew.

Suddenly, a red mist erupted in the dark morning's air. The streetlight illuminated the area as one of the attackers fell to the ground slumped, followed by the other, and Rob was finally able to rest where he laid. He closed his eyes and felt a fatigue like never before.

"Guess sleep's bitch ass still want a nigga." He smiled at his own amusing thought.

"Pop, get the car around here! He's hit and it looks bad!"

Those were the last words he heard as Gianna's pretty face appeared in his eyesight before darkness took over.

$ $ $ $ $

"Baby, Mack, get up!" Sylvia whispered as she shook her son hard once she was sure her paranoia wasn't getting the best of her.

"Wh-what's up, Ma?" he slurred, still groggy from a heavy slumber.

"There are shadows moving around outside and the silent alarm is buzzing like crazy," Sylvia whispered and signaled for him to keep his voice low. Her words sobered him up real quick and Aeriella jumped out of bed on the opposite side and quickly put her clothes on.

"Ma, y'all stay put," Young Mack rushed into his closet and grabbed the modified AR-15 he kept there with a hundred round drum connection. He quickly ran from the room and took the stairs two at a time to the bottom. The roaming lasers glowing outside the windows of their family home encouraged his haste. He quickly sprinted back up the stairs and grabbed the women and together, they hustled to get to the bottom of the stairs.

"Get to the basement, Ma, hurry!" Young Mack said as her feet touched the foyer's floor.

A huge blast blew through the front door and knocked the door off its hinges once Sylvia cleared its path. The pressure from the explosion threw Young Mack across the railing of the stairs and his weapon dropped from his hand. He struggled to make sense of what was going on around him as he collected his weapon and aimed it at the direction of the huge hole where their front door used to be. What happened next rocked his world, and it all played out in slow motion before his very eyes.

"Young Mack, are you okay?" He heard her voice before he saw her.

Beams swarmed the stairwell just as their eyes met and before he could order her to get down, one zoned in on the side of her face. Thinking quickly, he immediately swung his vision to the door and fired off round after round, dropping shit before they could penetrate the home. He scrambled to make it to Aeriella through the chaos as their home was being Swiss cheesed. He knew he was hit a few times because even though his adrenaline rushed, he could still feel the intense burning inside his body as he desperately made his way to where he last saw her looking down on him. All hope was lost once he saw her body sprawled out with blood all over her face. He stumbled and fell to his knees with blood running from his mouth, but nothing could stop him from getting to her. He needed her to be alright. She had to be for them to get married and create a family like he'd promised her. His strength faded as he pulled her body into his lap and rocked her softly until he was no longer conscious of anything going on around him. Anger filled his soul as he thought about the drama that unfolded around his life at a constant rate. He silently made a bargain to whomever could hear his prayers to spare his life now for his soul in the hereafter.

$ $ $ $ $

"Young Mack, Young Mack, baby, wake up, you're scaring me!" Aeriella shook him until he snapped back to life to the here and now.

"Wh-what the—— You're alive? Come here, ma. Damn, a nigga was already missing yo' ass!" He grabbed her up and squeezed her tight to his body. "I just had the wildest dream ever. I thought I lost you."

"Did the dream have anything to do with that?" Aeriella pointed to the flat screen on the wall.

It was then that his heart dropped to his stomach and gas threatened to erupt from a deep place inside of him. On the television was a breaking news coverage story of the Miller Estate attack. That's what the headline read as the reporter spoke, but her words couldn't be heard.

"Turn it up," he said, barely above a whisper.

Aeriella complied quickly. As she reached out to shorten the distance of the remote control's frequency, he saw all the bruising, cuts, and scrapes on her arm. He reached for her and a sharp pain erupted somewhere on his left side, causing his face to ball up, and a hiss escaped his lips.

"Fu——" His words were cut short when a sudden knock came upon the door to the room that he assumed to be a hospital room, but something caught his attention, and he was sure he wasn't tripping.

That hospital always smelled of pine oil, Lysol, and other disinfectants. This hospital room smelled different. It smelled like his mom's extravagant homemade Cajun gumbo. He'd smelled that smell all of his life growing up, loving the mixture of the Cajun soup over white rice and a side of crackers. He looked to Aeriella who noticed the confused look on his face.

"Fuck are we?"

"I was hoping that you could tell me," she replied softly with a nod towards the door.

He thought his eyes were playing tricks on him when he locked eyes with the very person he felt was responsible for the attack on his family's home.

"Nice to have you back with us." His voice was calm yet calculated.

Young Mack studied the man and watched his every move like a hawk. The ice grilled mug Young Mack gave the stranger alerted Aeriella, and she clutched the pocket knife she'd picked up that one of the armed guards had dropped the night before.

"Peace, my friend, I'm no enemy of yours."

"Jalamon, what the fuck are you doing here? Better yet, what the fuck are we doing here?"

"Watch yo' mouth, boy, there's women present!" Sylvia jovially stated as she glided across the room with a cooking apron on and a tray of what he already knew would be her special gumbo.

"These good people swooped in and saved your family, baby boy. Mama knows you're a man. Hell, you are the man. But it's always good for a man to show appreciation and respect at all times, even for his enemies. It'll give him the edge."

Young Mack's mood lightened from his mother's sense of humility. Seeing that all was well with her and paying close attention to the scars and bruises on his new fiancée, he knew there was a helluva lot to be thankful for. He reached out and rubbed the side of Aeriella's pretty face, where there was a bandaged cut above her right eyebrow. He fought to take his gaze away from her and looked towards the man responsible for pulling him and his girls out of hell.

His words caught up in his throat before he cleared it and thanked the man before him.

"You're absolutely welcome. Rest well now. There's a lot to discuss later," Jalamon stated.

"Of course there is," Young Mack stated with distaste.

He was never the one to like being in someone's debt, and as happy as he was that they made it outta the deadly attack, he still didn't wanna be indebted to anyone, nor did he trust anyone. The very thought of being indebted to Jalamon and his family made him think of the prayer he made when he thought it was all over for him and his girls. He shook his head and knew that he would uphold whatever it was that these people wanted of him.

"I know what you're thinking, and I assure you, that it's not the case. Only time will prove that to you. Now gather your strength. Business comes later," Jalamon sincerely spoke before closing the door behind him.

Chapter 12

"Can you believe this shit?" Drexler chuckled as he and his partner approached the disastrous scene.

"Yeah, but look who decided to leave their throne and join the regular people." Chandler nodded towards the director.

"No shit. Look at that shit!" Drexler shook his head.

Director Gamble arrived at the bullet-riddled mini mansion that looked like something out of an Al Pacino gangster movie. Busted windows, bullet holes in everything with a surface, front door blown in along with everything that held it together in place. There was a huge hole where the door should've been, and this once beautiful home now looked like a haunted house from old episodes of the show *Goosebumps*.

From a distance, Chandler knew that nothing good could come of such an attack, and he fully expected to see the guy the underworld cherished like the Godfather laid out with nothing of his soul left in his empty shell of a corpse. The forensic lab techs, the coroners and even the media scrambled about the property as the partners covered the massive front yard leading up to the main entrance of the home. It was then that they noticed the bodies sprawled out along the driveway up into the home.

"Sixteen dead in an all-out gun battle and none are Mackentosh Miller! Where is he? I want him found like yesterday!" Chandler heard the director yell into his personal cell phone as they approached him.

"Which one, sir?" Chandler said after clearing his throat to announce his and Drexler's presence.

"Neither one, as far as we know." Gamble suddenly ended his phone call without so much as telling the other person on the line goodbye. His actions were always suspicious when Chandler came around.

Chandler's detective tuition kept him on alert whenever he had to be around the director. He couldn't understand the acrid taste the director brought to his mouth, especially with them being on the same team. Or so his mind thought.

"What do we know so far?" Chandler asked as if his own investigation hadn't already begun.

"How about you mill around and talk to the workers all around that fall under your thumb, Agent? Do your job and we'll figure this thing out, but my brain ain't for your picking," Director Gamble stated before strolling away while yapping on his cell phone again.

"Rude prick. Man, don't sweat that one, partner, he's a real bitch boy at times," Drexler concluded about their boss.

"I'm not sweating that idiot, Drex, but something's up with him, I'm telling you. It's like he gets a stiffy every time he gets to address me like I'm less of an agent than I am."

"Wow, you're tooting your own horn again, and I'm starting to realize that I'm dealing with two dicks instead of one." Drexler shook his head while taking in one of the deadliest crime scenes he'd ever been to.

"I ain't tooting shit, dick. I'm calling it how I see it. There is some foul shit going on and I'm gonna get to the bottom of it, and then you'll be like, damn, partner, we sure showed them!" Chandler chuckled at his own humor.

"Oh yeah? And just how are you gonna do that, Brain?" Drexler mocked his partner's confidence.

"All the pieces to every puzzle begin together before they get taken apart for others to figure out how to put it back together. All the pieces are right where you can see them.

You just have to put them together, dick." Chandler nudged his partner to get his full attention. "Check it out."

"What the fuck?" Mackmillions bellowed once he laid eyes on his destroyed home and all the feds moving throughout his property.

$ $ $ $ $

Mackmillions couldn't believe his eyes as he rounded the corner where his home was located. News vans and reporters crowded both sides of the barricaded road leading up to his home. He had no choice but to get out on foot after taking it all in. His heart raced as he willed his feet to move at a quickened pace. The whispers and chatter from the thirsty news crews died out as they watched the nearly panic-stricken man make his way towards the officers and their barricades.

"Hold, sir, no one is allowed past this point." A bold field officer held his hand up for him to stop where he was.

"What's going on here?" Mackmillions was on the verge of breaking down.

"This is a restricted crime area, sir. Nothing more can be disclosed at this time, so if you're media, you need to back up and stand where the rest of them are," the same officer spoke.

"Media? This is my home. And what the fuck happened to my family? Where the hell is my family?" Mackmillions cleared the barrier before being apprehended by the two officers assigned to guard the barricade.

"Get the fuck off of me, mu'fuckas! Do y'all know who I am? Where is my family? All I want is my family!" Mackmillions fussed and fought to break free, but the officers didn't let up.

"Mackentosh Miller," Agent Chandler called out from above Mackmillions and the officers tussling on the ground.

"If you know who I am, then you know that's my residence over there."

"Yeah, well, what's left of it, that is." Drexler chuckled, but no one else saw the humor in his remark.

"Please tell me my family ain't dead, man. And get these two mu'fuckas up off of me!"

Agent Chandler thought for a minute before ordering the officers to release him. Chandler knew that in order for him to make any headway, he'd have to go with his gut and barrel into everything from the opposite direction, and being on Mackentosh Miller's good side definitely wouldn't hurt his situation.

"Good looking out. Damn, they got me all gritty and shit," Mackmillions stated while doing a stellar job at being a common thug.

"No problem. And to answer your question, no, your family wasn't found amongst the dead here, and I know as much as you. I gotta take you down to the station for questioning."

"Questioning? Bruh, I gotta find my family and figure out what the hell all this is about." Mackmillions was genuinely concerned about what happened at his home, but he knew for sure that his son and wife were more than capable of taking care of themselves and each other.

"Of course you do, and we'll have our people on it the entire time, but the questioning can't wait, as it could better assist us in our searches, especially for the ones involved in this carnage."

Agent Chandler absorbed all the energy in the room as he escorted the department's most sought after "alleged" crime lord. The streets loved him and praised him, and the many governmental agencies loved when they apprehended him. Even more, they loved when the trial court came back with the guilty verdict and one helluva long sentence. Now here he was in the flesh, and Chandler loved the attention they were getting, but of course, Agent Drexler could hardly wait to claim their celebrity status at the workplace.

"Watch out, big fish coming through!" Drexler capped to no one in particular as they made their way to the investigation chambers.

The chilled interrogation room was void of anything besides the long stainless-steel table and chairs. Dreaded stigma of the infamous interrogation rooms did nothing to Mackmillions. He smiled inside at how easily Agent Chandler had fallen into his reach. Sylvia had made contact with her husband the moment they were safely away from all the drama at the mansion and promised to update him on Young Mack's condition. Mackmillions feared that the hit was sent by players in the New Realm , but he had yet to figure it out for sure. The door opening and shutting brought him back to the cold, empty room and now the person standing before him.

"Well, well, if it isn't the big bad wolf himself," Director Gamble grumbled as he took a seat across from Mackmillions.

"Gamble," Mackmillions greeted the jealous and envious man.

Agent Chandler marveled at the difference in Mackmillions' posture and mannerisms. The low life persona was no longer in place and Chandler understood that Mackmillions was a man of many traits. The man before him looked way more calculated and collectively wise and a bit intimidating.

"You've been busy since your release, and I have to give it to you on the clean-ups," Gamble shot his shot prematurely.

"I'm sorry, I thought I was brought here to help with the safe return of my family. You know, to help bring in the termites that dismantled my home and died on my perfectly-manicured lawn," Mackmillions smiled slightly.

"Cut the bullshit, Mackentosh, nobody's listening, I've made sure of it." Gamble sat back in the steel chair and folded his arms across his chest.

It was true that he ordered everyone out of the listening room before he went in to talk to Mackmillions, but unbeknownst to him, Agent Chandler had other plans.

"There's no bullshit to cut, you egotistical bastard. I'm only here to help with my family and get down to the bottom of the attack on my home," Mackmillions stated, almost too calmly for Chandler to believe those words had just left his mouth.

"You're finished, you piece of shit. Everything you ever did in life will be erased from history once I'm finished with you. You think because it all began with you that it couldn't evolve into something way more promising and foolproof? Just accept your fate before your bloodline is ordered to extinction." Gamble loved the fact that he was getting the time to pester his prey.

"Did your boss order the hit on my family?" Mackmillions could feel his blood boiling while anticipating his answer.

"You know the answer to that, Mack, because none of your family was found there," Gamble stated with a smug expression, and the evil smirk made Mackmillions wanna crush his face.

"You have no idea what you're doing - none of you do - and it's sad how your ignorance seeps through your pink ,pungent pores. The crazy thing about it all is that as much as you think I care, I don't. What I do care about is why? Why wrongfully imprison me? All I've ever done was feed everyone, kept chaos and rodents out, and more importantly, I kept you all safe and out of the hands of pirate politicians. It was a crafty but uncalled for situation to have me taken away from my family, and it still angers me to the core that you greasy-handed cockroaches are able to suck up oxygen that you don't deserve forfeited by right." Mackmillions sat with his fingers clasped together atop the stainless-steel table.

A chill shot through the director once he noticed that there were no silver slave bracelets attached to his wrists.

"You may be right about the bogus imprisonment, but orders were given and actions had to be taken or death would have consumed us all. You know as well as anyone that the higher-ups make all the calls and it's outta our hands, and if they were willing to out you, then no one was safe. Now things are different for the lower levels. We've elevated our game and rained down on all that were above during your reign. We've cleansed heaven of the unworthy and deemed them all to live in the hell we've provided for them," Director Gamble stated before standing.

Mackmillions wanted to break the pig's neck and chop his body into hundreds of small pieces, then mail him to every member of the New Realm - family included.

"You'll never win, Gamble, and I pray that you've enjoyed your so-called reign of terror."

"I've already won, Mack. I'm director of the Bureau, if you haven't noticed. Not so bad for the once-square, wet-eared agent you knew, is it? Hell, I'm above the law, and the New Realm is here to stay." With that, Gamble smiled at the death stare Mackmillions was giving him while he made his exit.

Under different circumstances, Mackmillions would've killed that sour son of a bitch with his bare hands. He swore to himself to make him suffer tremendously when that time came for his death. Until then, he'd have fun killing them all and taking back what rightfully belonged to him. He shook his head and smiled at the red dot that appeared on his watch, indicating the tracker was live and in place. The sound of the door opening caught his attention, and he looked up to see the perplexed agent staring him down. Chandler steeped into the room and closed the door behind him.

"So, it's been you the whole time?" Chandler asked.

"Say what?" Mackmillions twisted his face up at the off-the-wall question.

"You can kill the act. I watched you two and I listened to everything," Chandler revealed.

"Fifteen years in federal max will do things to a man's vision." Mackmillions smiled at the eager agent.

"What does that have to do with anything?" Chandler asked, now confused.

"Cedrick Chandler, I was completely aware of your presence the entire time and I wanted you to listen and see for yourself with your own two eyes what you've questioned your entire life."

"My entire life? Duke, you don't know shit about me," Chandler growled.

"On the contrary. That's neither here nor there. Cedrick, this world is bigger than you and I both, and despite our different natures in life, as you can see, it's either eat or be eaten. I wouldn't be here if it wasn't time for you to choose a side."

"Wh——"

The door to the room slammed open and in walked an older Italian-looking brother dressed to the nines.

"Let's go, sir," the man stated before tossing the agent his card down on the table.

Mackmillions smiled. " Nice of you to show up. These nice people were trying to help me find my family."

"I bet. Only thing these filthy people will help you to find is a way back inside a cage," Early Estrada stated without emotion.

$ $ $ $ $

K-dawg stormed inside of the massive foyer of the Valdez estate, steaming. He was followed by Deuce, Rolla, Hogg, and surprising as anything, Ash. Young Mack smiled when he saw his guys enter and head straight over to check on him.

"Blood, you got me 'bout to bring the city to its knees!" K-dawg embraced his big homie. Young Mack meant the world to him and he was sure he could say the same for their entire operation.

"Good to see you too, fam. It's good to see all of you here safe and sound." Young Mack embraced them all with handshakes and hugs.

"You know we on it as soon as you say go," Hogg stated with a heart laced in venom.

"Fo' shit sho," Deuce and Rolla agreed.

Young Mack was proud that Rolla had come along because he was everything that K-dawg said that he was, and Young Mack was big on loyalty.

"On life, we'll get to that. But I brought you boys out here to Mexico for more than one reason."

"K-dawg, how are you, son?" Sylvia greeted the only one of her son's men that she was familiar with.

"I'm Gucci now that I know he's good. But how about you, queen?" K-dawg saluted his mentor's mother.

"Ma, I was about to explain to the fellas why I brought them all this way." Young Mack smiled at his mother.

"Well, you guys are about to step up to the next level in the game, a level that many can wish for, but only some can acquire," Sylvia stated.

"You mean like on some cartel shit like in the urban novels I read while I was in the bing?" Deuce asked joyfully.

"Yeah, only this is real life and we can't have mercy on the streets all across America. That hood love is out the window. We're products of the environment, but now we're gonna be the ones controlling shit." Young Mack took a sip from a tasteful drink put together by Stephanie.

He noticed her watching how he addressed his crew and she loved the way he demanded attention with his calm and calculated demeanor. He smiled and winked at her.

"How are we supposed to do that when we've been on the scrap tryna keep shit afloat in the city? Then we got a lot of bodies to lay down after what just happened in your homeland," K-dawg asked.

"Steph, come here, ma!" Young Mack waved her over.

The guys watched as the beautiful and seductive Spanish woman made her way over at Mack's beckoning. Her skin was kissed bronze and her hair was silky black and flowed past her waist. They all watched her with their mouths agape.

"Hola. I'm Stephanie Valdez. Welcome to my home and country," she wooed them with the skill of a veteran seductress.

"Shit just got a whole lot better!" K-dawg laughed as he took every bit of her in.

"Fellas, I'm Miguel, this is my younger brother Jalamon, and you've just met my younger sister." Miguel smiled at their obvious lust-filled gazes at his sister. Her beauty was her deadliest attribute.

"We have a lot to discuss now that you're here, but we'll allow you guys to enjoy our home and get settled in before we get into that. Everything you need will be met by our staff, and might I add that our maids are at your beck and call twenty-four hours a day," Jalamon spoke up before tapping his brother's shoulder, and both of them walked away as quietly as they came.

"Fellas, Stephanie will answer any questions about our stay here if any of you have any. Ash, I need to get at you. Come on this way." Young Mack led the way into the expansive room he shared with his fiancée, who sat looking amazing as she talked with her mother via Facetime.

Young Mack took a seat next to her on the king-sized bed and waited for her to end her call before making the introduction between her and Ash, then got down to the business of why he invited him into their room away from everybody else.

"Ash, you know I love you like a brother I never had, right?" Young Mack decided to take a soft approach to such a delicate conversation.

"Fo' shit sho, same here, but what's going on?"

"I'm about to tell you something that may change our relationship forever, but I gotta give it to you like it is."

"Well, let's hear it, and let me be the judge of that," Ash stated, eager to hear what had Young Mack so disturbed.

"I've been sleeping with Ambrea for nearly as long as we've been friends." Young Mack paused and Ash remained silent as he looked on dumbfoundedly.

"That's it?" Ash questioned, not fazed by the news in the least bit.

"You're not mad at me for that?" Young Mack was genuinely surprised by Ash's reaction.

"I've known that since like forever, Mack. My sister doesn't keep anything away from me. She didn't want you to tell me because she wanted to protect our friendship in case you two ever fell out, and I respect you even more for honoring her wishes. I don't look at it as you betraying me by keeping it from me," Ash shockingly revealed.

"Damn, y'all hid that shit so good!" Young Mack laughed and brought a smile to everyone's face.

After filling Ash in on everything that transpired and explaining where he was needed, they reentered the entertainment area of the Valdez's mansion.

"Nice to see everyone getting along, but we need to get down to business," Young Mack made his presence known in the room.

K-dawg, whose shirt was off, as usual, poised himself on the side of the expensively hand-crafted pool table before taking his best shot. Everyone watched as the cue ball jumped around the table and avoided contact with the striped balls idly sitting in its path before colliding with the black eight ball and knocking it into the corner pocket.

"Easy money!" K-dawg boasted as he blew powder from the tip of his pool stick.

Miguel smiled in astonishment as K-dawg sank the game winning ball into the leather pocket to beat his sister. She'd reigned over him and Jalamon for years, and to watch her lose was bittersweet.

"Lucky win," Stephanie stated before sashaying over to the bar and reaching over into her two-hundred-thousand-dollar Hermes Birkin bag and retrieving a wad of bills before tossing them across the room to K-dawg.

"Ain't nothing lucky about the dawg, ma!" K-dawg chuckled as he fanned through the crisp bills.

Stephanie rolled her eyes at the cocky youngster and stepped face to face with Young Mack. Ever since he stepped into the room, demanding the attention of everyone, she felt a tingling on her hardening clitoris.

"Engaged to be married, huh?" she asked, rubbing her soft hands over his toned chest down to his six pack abs.

"Problem?" he asked, looking deep into her seductive portals.

"Nooo, I'm very good at keeping secrets, plus with as much power as my family is providing you with, I have to watch over and protect our investment." She smiled before grabbing a handful of his semi-erection through the material of his Gucci linens and kissing the corner of his lips.

Young Mack was amused by the sexy queenpin as she wiped her lip print from his mouth and stepped around him, sure that all of their eyes would be plastered on her natural derriere. Yount Mack watched his men ogle her with lustful eyes.

Miguel looked to Jalamon and Jalamon to Miguel before both their stares fell back on Young Mack in appraisal. They had watched infamous leaders of huge drug cartel factions in their country and those in countries around the world fall into the seductions of their younger sister, yet Young Mack didn't seem the least bit drawn by her attempts on him. Both brothers felt honored to have the young man on their side. He was focused and determined, and they now shared a common enemy.

"First order of business is getting y'all faces outta her ass and getting y'all minds on operations." Young Mack took a seat at the wet bar.

"Damn, my bad, bro." K-dawg laughed and got nothing in return but a hard stare.

"It's time we take it to the city in a major way, then after that, we take it to every city aligned in the southern states. We conquer the south, move west, then work our way east." Young Mack had it all plotted out in his mind, and with the help of the third largest cartel family in Mexico, he knew that his field of vision could be very wide.

"I like the way you think, but that would be one treacherous and deadly mountain to climb, not to mention nearly impossible, for that matter." Miguel laughed at the overzealous youngster.

"What do you have in mind?" Jalamon believed in Young Mack. Not only did he have faith in him, so did his sister, and he knew the powers of her mind's eye. Unbeknownst to everyone, he visited the hundred-and-three-year-old oracle, a source that not too many knew about, and the knowledgeable elder told him, "You follow the black wolf, for he is surely a worthy guide."

"I am going to kill Gurdo," Young Mack confessed.

$ $ $ $ $

"So this is the place?" Mackmillions asked as he sat accompanied by Max and KenKen in a tinted-out Benz sprinter van.

"Absolutely this is it," KenKen replied, sure of himself.

"It betta be, fa ya health!" Max stated, only half-trusting anything that came outta KenKen's mouth.

Max was a natural born killer since birth, and murder had been his only hustle and favorite sport. There was no doubt in his mind that if he sensed anything outta pocket, he'd kill KenKen first before anyone else.

"Look, man, fuck off with all yo' threats, gee. I ain't running from no death fight, not even from the devil himself when it's my turn to go. I'm here because I wanna be here and I'd rather not be dead, so if I'm saying that this is one of the five stashes, then that's exactly what that is," KenKen defended himself.

"First thing first, you're gonna get us into the building, being that you're still under oath with the Realm. Secondly, you're gonna open the rear entrance for Max and me and we'll ambush the whole joint with these bulletproof suits and fully automatic rifles."

Mackmillions formed a weapon with his hands and pretended to shoot up the place. And that's exactly what they did. Gaining entry was easy for KenKen, like he knew it would be, and that was one reason why he planned to rob the spot himself one day. Now he stood by watching as Mackmillions and his sick goon tortured man after man for every piece of intel they had on the New Realm's operations.

"AAAAARRRGH!" the last victim screamed out as Max squeezed his throat before crushing his trachea with a fatal amount of pressure.

"I'll get the van, Max. You and KenKen load it while I take care of the security feed," Mackmillions ordered.

"Never mind that, because we only have minutes to get all this money into that van and be out," KenKen warned.

"Minutes? What do you mean?" Mackmillions asked.

"These cameras don't save footage. They're watched from live feed."

"Shit!" Mackmillions humped to get down to loading the van.

Bag after bag after bag they rushed to get the undisclosed amount of money into the van before burning rubber out of the building, colliding into the security SUV rushing to put a stop to their escape.

"Max, go live!" Mackmillions ordered, and that he did.

Max expertly finger-fucked the trigger on his Specter M-4 submachine gun, knocking meat and bone fragments from every passenger of the security vehicle before they could fire off a single shot.

"Look, there's more coming!" KenKen yelled as Mackmillions backed the wrecked sprinter away from the security vehicle before going around it.

KenKen nearly panicked once Mackmillions threw him the OTs 33 Pernach select fire handgun he'd admired from their expansive arsenal of weapons. The fact that Mackmillions actually brought the gun after denying him a weapon earlier made him bust his gun even harder as the vehicle sped towards them.

Burst after burst erupted form the .9MM's three round select as the gun hopped up and then back in KenKen's grip. Sparks flew from the bulletproof metal of the New Realm's hitters Benz truck that was being followed by a matte black Land Rover.

"Tires!" Mackmillions yelled as he stepped from the driver's seat, holding a H&K MP5K equipped with a grenade launcher and a carbon fold stock.

KenKen was successful with his aim as the front driver side tire exploded and the truck whooped to one side just as they began firing shots from their lowered passenger windows. Hollows pierced the night's air, striking the sprinter continuously until the truck swerved in an attempt to stop the expensive 4WD, with little to no success. The brakes hissed and fluid spewed before catching fire after contacting sparks from the blown tire. All the doors flew open as the truck streamlined its way towards the concrete structure yards away.

Max pounced from behind the security vehicle and fired with twin Beretta 39Rs, striking target after target. Shots were wildly returned, but Max came from a blind spot, shooting accurately as an assassin on a mission. He dropped all four passengers before the truck crashed into the wall.

Mackmillions was under heavy fire and couldn't get a shot off at the armored SUV. Max quickly changed things after firing his last rounds at the Land Rover. They immediately changed directions and took aim before corralling hollows towards Max, who dove for cover behind the downed security vehicle. Mackmillions rose to one knee once he was sure his chance was open and dumped around at the bottom of the Land Rover. It only took seconds for two of the shooters to propel towards the sky once the explosion lifted everything in the air. Mackmillions dumped another round into the cabin from the open back passenger window. Smoke and fire followed the explosion, and the reeking smell of burnt flesh wafted through the night's air.

"Max, you good?" Mackmillions called out.

"Good!" Max replied, then rose from his low spot on the ground.

"KenKen, talk to me." Mackmillions approached their ride.

"All good," KenKen spoke up before rising with two weapons trained on Mackmillions and Max. Max then raised both of his weapons, ready to rock KenKen into an eternal sleep.

"You're empty." KenKen smiled as Max lowered his weapons.

"I'm not," Mackmillions said with his weapon aimed at KenKen's face.

"Whoa, chill out, man, the money is in here!" KenKen shouted while holding the empty weapons in the air to show them that no clips were locked into place. "I was just fucking around so I could get you to let me keep a weapon. I put in work here too, you know."

"By doing that?" Mackmillions chuckled at the balls on KenKen. "You're lucky if Max lets you keep your arms."

Mackmillions jumped into the passenger seat and tossed his weapon in the back with the bags of stolen money.

KenKen looked to Mackmillions with wide eyes before putting the sprinter van into drive.

"You'd let him do that to me?" KenKen asked, shocked.

"Shut up and drive, Ken, we're good." Mackmillions laughed.

Chapter 13

Gianna could never get used to the constant chirping of the machines helping her man hold on to his life. It was one thing to see him all bandaged up, yet another to see him with so many tubes running in and out of his body. It was breaking her down knowing she couldn't protect him when she should have been right there with him.

The sound of the hospital door opening pulled her attention away from her self-hate. She sighed once she made eye contact with Rob's mother Mary as she stepped into the room. Mary was always a joy to be around, and Gianna needed her presence now more then she would ever admit.

"How is he?" Mary asked in her usual calm and soft voice.

"Nothing much has changed since he made it out of surgery nearly ten hours ago," Gigi informed her while looking him over.

"I hate hospitals," Mary honestly admitted before sitting down lightly on the side of her son on his hospital bed. She lightly rubbed her fingers over the skin of his cheeks before placing the back of her hand on his forehead to check his temperature. Satisfied with her findings, she stood and kissed his cheek before moving over to sit next to Gianna on the small sofa situated underneath the room's window. "How are you, baby?" Mary could see the stress lines in her face.

The tell-tale bags under her eyes showed that she hadn't been getting any sleep. "Worried. I'm worried about him,

Ms. Mary. I need for him to pull through and remember who we are," Gianna confessed.

"Gianna, baby, let Allah worry about that and how he wants things to be. Whether he loses little or all of his memory, it will be our job to see to it that he's good, and we'll do that without a shadow of a doubt. I may not know my son as well as a mother should, but one thing I do know, and that's a man's love. And when I look at you and him together, all I see is the love you two share because it radiates, and everyone around you can see it plain and clear."

"Yes ma'am, I'm with you on that." Gianna smiled a weak smile. Fatigue was kicking her ass, and she knew she needed to get some rest before she blacked out.

"Baby you need to get some rest. I can see that you're tired and I'm here now. I'll watch over him and keep you safe while you sleep." Mary patted her Hermes Birkin clutch to assure her that she was indeed packing.

"I guess I should get a few hours in, but you wake me as soon as the doctor comes," Gianna requested.

"Will do," Mary promised.

Gianna was out cold and slightly snoring in less than five minutes. Mary searched the hospital room until she found a clean folded-up woven blanket in the bathroom's closet. After tucking Gianna in, she silently made her way back to her son's bed and said a soft prayer over his head.

"Hump, hump, hey Ma," Rob spoke in a raspy voice as his words scratched their way through his dry throat.

"God has been good to you, son." Mary smiled while rubbing her son's chest.

"Water," Rob spoke just above a whisper. The pressure suddenly brought on a throbbing headache. "Ahhh, ahh."

"Wait, baby, let me take care of you," Gianna said, surprising both Rob and Mary, who thought she was sleep.

Gianna moved with haste, filling up a glass of mildly cold tap water, and added a straw for him to drink from. After making sure he drank a fair share from the glass, she reached beside his bed and hit the call button for the nurses to step in.

"I'm so glad that you pulled through," Gianna said with both hands clasped together and pressed against her lips. She watched him through teary eyes as he looked her over and she instantly began to worry. "You don't remember me, do you?"

"What? Woman, stop being dramatic and get over here and kiss these lips.," Rob smiled weakly.

"That's what I'm talking about." Gianna smiled and laid her head on his chest after kissing his lips time and time again.

"She hasn't left this room since you made it out of surgery, son." Mary smiled as she was proud of the support Gigi was showing him.

"She saved my life, Ma." Rob's memory shot him back to the moment in time when Gigi blew the brains out of the attacker before he could advance on him in his weakened state.

"Surely did," the proud black doctor said as she stepped into the room followed by two nurses, one male and one female. "Hi, I'm Dr. Essien. Glad to have you back so soon. That is a great sign for sure."

"Doc, I need something for my head, because my shit is killing me since those shells didn't," Rob admitted.

"Of course it is, son. We just pulled a whole bullet from it." Dr. Essien removed a drip bag from her overcoat and handed it to the female nurse to hook it up.

"Baby, are you okay?" Gigi asked.

"A bullet from my skull?" Rob asked while reaching up to touch his bandaged head. The sound of the vital machine beeped as his heart rate increased intensely.

"Son, you have to calm down," Mary said, near panicked.

"Don't worry yourself. He'll be out before you can snap your fingers." And boy, was the doctor on point with her assessment.

"Thanks, Doctor," Mary stated sincerely.

"No thanks needed here. He's a true sport, and I'm sure he'll be okay once the headaches subside. Plus there will possibly be blackout spells for a few months, but we'll be cautious as to what types of meds to put him on.

"Blackout spells?" Monsta interrupted the doctor, as he and Pop entered the room.

"Shut up!" Pop elbowed his younger brother.

"Once again, thank you, Doctor, for everything," Mary reiterated her appreciation.

"You're absolutely welcome, and if there is anything you all may need, the nurses will be here to take care of you every half hour like clockwork." Dr. Essien smiled and waved goodbye to everyone before leaving, followed by her helpers.

"Damn, I wonder if she's a cougar," Monsta whispered to his brother, who looked him over as if he were crazy.

"How are you doing, Ms. Mary?" Pop asked after dismissing his brother.

"I'm fine, thank you, and so is your partner over there. Gigi, Pop, Monsta…we need to talk about what happened with my son," Mary stated before taking a seat.

"Straight ambush at the house. They came to kill for sure, and we were able to rock all that were sent - with Rob's help, of course. He didn't go down until it was all done, and I saw the bullet when it ricocheted and went in his direction. I just never thought it hit him until he just laid down as if he was tired, and that's when I knew something was wrong," Gianna explained everything as she saw it happen.

"Do we know which one of my son's enemies were responsible for the attack?"

"I believe I do one hundred percent," Gigi replied.

"You do?" Monsta interjected.

"I want blood, Gianna. I know who you are, and the two of you also, and I know what my husband had planned for the three of you and my deceased son. I have money - more money than I could possibly spend in two lifetimes, - I want the three of you to build a team of the grimiest and most savage men and women you can find. I've already lost too much, and I'm simply tired of it. You will build this team in support of my son Robert and for his protection, but for me, you will seek out and destroy those responsible for the murder of my son and my husband. No expense is too much for this task," Mary pointed out.

"But what about the homie's approval of this?" Monsta stated with a head nod towards a sleeping Rob.

"He'll be out of it for a spell, but you leave him to me," Mary replied.

"Oh, it's definitely on now!" Monsta slightly elbowed his brother in excitement. If they never had agreed on anything in life, murder was a definite exception.

$ $ $ $ $

"How could you have missed a sitting target, Daniel?" Gurdo asked in a calm but irritated voice.

"The little shit had help from outside sources. My men watched that place, and it had no security detail in place, so how was I to know that someone would swoop in and help him at a time like that?" Daniel was heated about the whole failed mission but like he said, there was no way for him to know things would turn out the way that they did.

"Pops is mad as shit at the huge loss of manpower on a mission for someone that isn't even a threat. He nearly bitched me out behind it until Mom came to my rescue because he continues to try to micromanage the family business from the bench like he's not even retired. It makes me sick too and I almost lost it at dinner because he put me in charge of the family operation, so I'll run shit how I see fit." Gurdo finished twisting a thick blunt of haze and put fire to it.

170

There was so much going on around him and their business that he refused to allow his father to get to him. Not that he didn't value his father's personal opinion and wisdom, because there was no comparison to anything he valued more than that he just wanted his father to allow him to be his own man and to run things his way. Daniel knew all too well how sensitive the subject was for his best friend and decided to lighten the blow a little.

"Dad is right, you know. I fucked up. But it's not on you, it's on me, and I'll be sure to verbalize that to him as soon as possible."

"Thanks, but there's no need for that, plus I want the situation to pass with him because you know how he is when something is on his mind." Gurdo waved him off and handed him the blunt.

The two of them worshipped the time they got to relax with each other and just kick back with kush and liquor at their disposal.

"We've come a long way from little pissant little boys running around terrorizing our neighbors and dad's business associates," Daniel reminisced.

"Most definitely so, and that's why I'm calling the hit off on the black kid," Gurdo confessed.

The news shocked Daniel, and he choked on the potent smoke. His head was on spin and he had to sit down and rest his head back until shit stopped spinning around so fast.

"I take it that you don't like the idea?" Gurdo concluded.

"Fuck no. Now it's like you're being dad to me," Daniel brought his feelings to light.

"It's not that, brother, but I completely understand your viewpoint. But you said it yourself that Pops is right, and he wants our attention on business and running the family in all the Texas cities now and not just keeping our focus on Houston."

171

This was also news to Daniel, and the smile on his best friend's face was a clear indication that he knew this news would excite him.

"All of the cities are ours now? Are you shitting me?"

"With the help of Mom, we got 'em all, brother."

They were both excited, for this was a challenge they'd both embarked on since the organization was handed down to them.

"That's what the fuck I'm talking about!" Daniel was indeed excited.

"Baby, where are you!" Ambrea shouted after entering their home after a long day out shopping and pampering with her friends and sisters-in-law.

"Psssh," Daniel blew a breath in irritation.

It was no secret to anyone that Daniel had it out for his best friend's wife. In his eyes, she had betrayed their trust, and he couldn't understand how Gurdo could forgive and forget so easily. He wasn't the one fucking her, so he didn't feel the need to do either ever.

"Calmate, cabron, ella es mi esposa." Gurdo warned his brother form another mother to calm down when speaking towards his wife."I'm out here, love!" Gurdo shouted to let her know where to find him.

"Oh, here you are, handsome." Ambrea smiled seductively after laying eyes on her husband for the first time all day.

"You looking delicious, mami." Gurdo smiled as she catwalked her way over to him before sitting on his lip and kissing his lips.

"I love you," she admitted honestly while wiping gloss from his lips with her thumb.

"Love you too, baby. Aren't you going to speak to Daniel?" Gurdo smiled because he loved being the instigator between the two people he loved more than anything outside of his immediate family.

"For what? All he's going to do is say something stupid like I'm one of his floozies and make me wanna slap his ass," Ambrea stated without acknowledging Daniel and keeping her eyes locked with those of her husband.

"You're so lucky he loves you, chica, or I'd erase your entire bloodline." Daniel smiled devilishly.

"I'd pipe down with all those phony threats because you're not the only one with deadly intentions, mutherfucker. I'd make it my life's mission to hunt down every family member that has ever even as much as touched your sick ass and kill everyone's kids first," Ambrea stated in all seriousness.

"Is that a challenge? Because I promise I'm faster." Daniel sat forward at the mention of his kids and their mothers.

"Come on now, both of you kill that noise, because neither of you are doing shit to harm each other. Respect the fact that I'm sitting right here and both of you are speaking about harming people that I love and care for!" Gurdo raised his voice in frustration while instantly regretting saying anything in the first place to spark the two of them. He hated the twist of events that brought them to hate one another when they used to be so close.

"I'm sorry, baby, but I told you how he's been acting towards me lately," Ambrea apologized.

"Can you honestly blame him?" Gurdo continued to snap before he could catch himself.

The look she gave him hurt him, and he knew he'd fucked up majorly. Their relationship had stood the test of time and trials, yet he'd just opened the wounds that easily. Tears immediately flooded her eyes and she moved out of his lap before he could have the satisfaction of seeing her cry.

"Baby, I'm sorry I said that." Gurdo reached for her waist.

"Don't touch me!" Ambrea swatted his hands away and stormed inside.

"Let her go, brother. She's soft," Daniel stated while putting fire back to the blunt they were smoking.

Gurdo slapped the blunt from his hand after he tried to pass it to him.

"Fuck was that?" Daniel shouted while rising from his seat.

Gurdo followed suit and stood toe to toe with him. The two of them stood nearly identical in their six-foot stature and muscle mass.

"You're gonna fuck around and be the cause of me losing my wife, idiot, and I'll never forgive you if that happens."

Daniel immediately felt sorry for going at Ambrea, even though he knew deep down that his best friend felt the way that he did about her supposed betrayal.

"You're right, and I'll do my best to fix it, brother."

Daniel stepped around his man in pursuit of Ambrea to apologize for both their actions. He moved through the house, listening closely to pinpoint her location. He found her in their master bedroom and knocked softly on the door before trying the handle which was locked.

"Go away! I don't wanna see you right now!" Ambrea yelled out.

"It's me, sis," Daniel stated before things got silent on the other side of the door.

It had been a long time since he'd referred to her as his sister, and he knew he'd soften her up with that approach. Or so he thought. Ambrea snatched the door open and his eyes grew into the size of dinner plates when he saw the huge handgun aimed between his eyes.

"You stupid or what, bitch? Coming in here like shit's sweet calling me your sister and shit!" she growled with anger and tear-soaked eyes.

"Calm down, woman," Daniel tried, but she wasn't going.

"Fuck you, mutherfucker! I swear if I lose my husband because of your sorry ass, I'm gonna kill you and everything you love, and you can try me by trying something stupid right here, right fucking now!"

Gurdo rushed into the hallway once he heard the yelling and stopped in his tracks once he saw what was happening.

"Baby, what are you doing?" he asked calmly without taking another step.

Unbeknownst to Daniel, Gurdo knew that his wife was trained to go and had witnessed her kill, and he knew she'd spray his brains across the wall behind him.

"He's making you hate me, and I haven't done anything wrong Gurdo!" Her emotions were everywhere.

"What are you saying? I don't hate you, and I know you have not done anything wrong. Now I'm sorry that I yelled and said that shit earlier. I was just heated at you two going at each other like that," Gurdo said in all honesty.

"I'm not some little weak-ass bitch like you think and I've given you time to get shit outta your system yet you choose to continue to try my hand, Daniel. I don't care if you feel any kind of disrespected by this or if it makes you wanna kill me because you've been doing that to me for weeks now. Whereas I used to love you and respect you, now I hate you too and don't like you anymore, so bring whatever my way and I promise I'll prove to you that I'm way deadlier than you or any of your enemies!" And with that, she lowered her weapon, looked to her husband, then turned on her designer heels and slammed their bedroom door before locking it to let Gurdo know that she was still pissed at him too.

"Damn, what just happened?" Gurdo asked no one in particular.

"Boss, we have a big problem!" One of Gurdo's security men rushed in and stopped beside him in the hallway.

"Big problem?" Gurdo asked just before a big explosion rattled his home. "What the fuck was that?"

Daniel lifted his leg and kicked in the door to Gurdo's bedroom with one hard boot. Ambrea jumped out of bed with her weapon trained on the door.

"Wait, it's me, babe!" with both hands up in surrendering fashion.

"Stay here, both of you, until I make it back for you. No matter what, don't leave this room unless you go into the situation room, and I'll look for you there if we need to escape," Daniel rattled off, filled with adrenaline.

"Be safe, brother." Gurdo pounded his fist over his best friend's chest.

"No sweat, brother, you know I live for these moments." Daniel smiled and returned Gurdo's gesture before rushing out and into the action.

Daniel rushed to one of the hidden compartments in the wall of Gurdo's crib and quickly retrieved two .9MM handguns with extended clips, two extra clips for his weapons, and a special edition M-16 crossed with an AR-15 hybrid with a scope and beam modification.

"Pussies want it with us, then let's get it!" he said to himself.

He couldn't believe his eyes once he stepped outside and rounded the pavilion towards the front of the estate. Security vehicles were in flames. Three of their men had lost their lives, and shots were being fired in rapid successions from both sides.

"Fuck!" Daniel breathed a sigh of relief when a round clinked into the metal of one of the vehicles next to him. He lifted his assault rifle, eyed the scope, and quickly located a target, then released a single round that exploded the guy's forehead like a pumpkin thrown into a wall at full force. "Bitch!"

Daniel felt a strong pain in his left shoulder as his adrenaline carried him further into action. He moved deathly while delivering fatal shots to their attackers, who were trying their best to enter the grounds of the estate through the double-reinforced doors that held up and stood the pressure.

"Keep those bitches on the other side of that gate!" Daniel yelled his orders to his men in Spanish as he continued to help hold the opposition at bay.

Shots abruptly erupted from the other side of the mansion and Daniel immediately knew that they were breached. He dropped his assault rifle before removing both handguns from his back and breaking into a full sprint. He rounded the house just as three masked men scaled the wall, then removed their weapons. Daniel sent shots their way and halted their advance as he made his way into the home through the back door with rounds bearing into the stucco walls at head level on his trail. He could feel the presence of the mask men as he ran full speed while sending shots backwards blindly. A muffled groan and thud ensured him that he'd gotten one of them. He rushed inside of the master bedroom and to the situation room secretly stashed behind one of the walls in the room. Behind the wall sat a large safe room whereas they could watch the intruders through the two-way mirror installed there. The intruders frustrations were apparent and their masks came off exposing to Daniel what he would've never imagined.

"Where the fuck did he go?" Deuce yelled in anger.

The shell he'd taken to the vest from the coward running and shooting backwards hurt like hell.

"Check this house from top to bottom and kill everything you come in contact with," Young Mack ordered, and his men left the room in haste.

Young Mack walked around the room as the scent of jasmine invaded his nostrils. It was a scent he knew all too well because Ambrea loved the scent of jasmine.

"I know you're in there, pussies!" Young Mack teased with a devilish grin. "I also know about the safe room and the bulletproof glass here!" Young Mack fired a shot that ricocheted off the glass window.

Daniel jumped in reflex and gritted his teeth in seething anger. Young Mack laughed at the irony of the situation.

"You bitches tried to kill the wrong mu'fucka, and now I won't stop until I bring you to your knees, Gurdo!" Young Mack fired another ricocheting shot at the glass. "I know you're in there, and you better listen closely, bitch! I knew I'd miss you this time, but I also knew I'd get your attention fo' shit sho, so thank your wife for my empathy this time. Just know that nothing remains the same from this point on and I need you to know I'm coming for your entire operation, bitch boy, until there's nothing left to remember you by!" Young Mack revealed, then turned to leave but stopped in his tracks at the door. "Daniel boy, I'll be seeing you real soon, and I promise you a surprise you'll never forget!" Young Mack laughed before tossing a single grenade below the window he knew they were watching him from before racing out of there.

Chapter 14

Gianna inhaled a long pull from the exotic mixture of kush and cocaine before exhaling and immediately embraced the rush, not to mention the tingling she felt between her legs that always came from her getting high. She and Monsta sat waiting patiently up the block from their target's mini mansion as Pop and two savage bitches Gianna brought along for the mission did their thing on the inside.

"You sure we can trust these bitches?" Monsta asked for the hundredth time.

Gianna stared at him with glossy red eyes lowered into slits. He was very irritating at times, but she had grown used to it over the years of being around him. He could tell from the look in her eyes that she was toasted and immediately knew two things. One, she was about to get on some real savage shit with whomever their victims were about to be, and secondly, he knew she was horny and wet as a pool.

"I'm buggin', ma, that's my bad," he apologized, then placed his hand on her silky thigh.

The shorts she wore were riding high and he could see the fat puff of her pussy perfectly. He moved his hand tenderly over her hot skin and she watched on without saying a word before his big-handed fingers made contact with her middle.

"Don't," she moaned, but didn't try to stop him because the sensation felt so good.

"I got'chu, ma. You know it's been a minute since you let me hit this pussy." Monsta moved the material of her shorts out of the way before running his fingers through the leg and through her panties.

"Shiiitt," Gigi moaned as her juices soaked his fingers once they entered her tight pussy.

"That's it, ma, ride them bitches until you pop that nut, and think about how I'm finna pound that pussy and bust that fat ass once we go in here and kill up some shit." Monsta knew all the things to say to her and he was glad that he did.

The mention of his pound game set a fire inside of her as she felt her orgasm build pretty quickly, but the mentioning of killing shit rocked her core and her juices squirted out as he continued to assault her tunnel and circle her clit simultaneously.

"Fuck, Monsta, you bogus as shit for that!" Gianna said while trying to catch her breath and fix her clothes.

Monsta sucked his fingers, then licked the palm of his right hand where her juices had pooled up. "Don't taste like it, and you sure did a great job of tryna stop me." He laughed cockily.

"Fair warning, Monsta: don't ever take advantage of me while I'm high again," she warned.

"Shut up, bitch, you know my get down and you ain't scaring shit." He waved her off.

"I'm with someone now and you better respect that shit, or I'll cut yo' dick off and feed it to yo' bitch ass." Gigi was dead serious. She knew she was wrong for letting him touch her, but she needed the nut with Rob still recovering, and her high had her gone.

"Whatever." He waved her off again as he looked at his phone, waiting for a coded text from his brother.

Gianna reached into the back seat for a change of bottoms. Just as she found something, Monsta's phone chimed, alerting them it was time to go.

"Let's go!" He looked her over as she stretched her body over the back seat and stared at her fat ass.

Gianna knew what he was doing, but fuck it. It wasn't like he'd never had it before, and she knew he wouldn't be getting it again as long as she was with Rob. In her mind, she knew she had to check him on his behavior before he got too outta hand and jeopardized both of their positions.

"I'll just put these on over my shorts, since you seem to lack manners."

"Whatever, ma, let's go," he replied, then climbed out of the passenger side with his fully-loaded Colt 635 sub slung over his shoulder. He then checked the extended clips for his fully automatic Beretta.9MM and smiled once the copper casings shined from the illumination of the streetlight positioned ten yards ahead of them.

"I'm ready," Gigi said without breaking her stride towards their destination.

Pop stood quietly watching the festivities going on around him. What started out as a night of friendly drinking, eating, and recreational games had now turned out to be a kush smoking fuck session. The orgy popped off shortly after Pop had the savage sisters tamper with everyone's drinks, overloading them with Percs and mollies. The men couldn't keep their hands off of Pop's guests, two of Gigi's tattooed savages, and their women couldn't keep their hands off of each other while they watched their men fuck the shit outta the beautiful women.

"Fuck, papi, you're deep in my stomach!" Misty, one half of the duo, screamed and faked an orgasm.

"Sis, he's fucking my asshole apart!" Stormy yelled, but unlike her sister, she wasn't faking.

Dude was really getting to his business, and as much as she hated to end their heated romp, she knew the time was coming for her to step to her business.

"I'ma cum in this tight culo, mami, you ready?" the tall, muscular guy asked as his load readied for her.

"That's enough!"

Everyone stopped after hearing the unfamiliar voice interrupt them.

"Wh——" the tall guy started, but never got to finish his statement before Pop connected a haymaker to his chin, knocking him out cold.

"Hey, puto, what the fuck?" The other guy jumped up and out of Misty's wet pussy with his small dick dripping on the plush carpeted floor.

"Shut him up," Gigi ordered, and Misty leaped from the floor behind him and connected a devastating roundhouse kick, snapping his head to his shoulder, knocking him out cold as well.

Gianna looked to the two women hugged up on the couch looking on in horror. She knew the women. Hell, all five of them grew up in the same streets together up until high school where it all changed for Gigi and ultimately their girl gang.

"Let's have fun with these bitches!" Monsta looked up to his big brother, who was standing over him as he zip tied both the unconscious men.

Pop couldn't lie and say he wasn't horny as hell after watching all that action before his brother and Gianna arrived.

"Gigi, how we playing this?" Pop asked, also eyeing the naked women with lust.

"Do 'em dirty," Gigi ordered.

Memories flooded her from her childhood of the tormenting trio. She loved the look in Brandi's eyes before she delivered the death blow with the pick axe after she'd done everything Gigi asked her to.

"Told you bitches y'all couldn't fuck with my business," Gigi mumbled as she watched Pop and Monsta destroy them.

Almost an hour after her men had finished with the women, she had them wake the men from their slumber.

"Wake up, bitches!" Monsta yelled, then threw steaming hot water on them.

Both men woke up screaming obscenities in Spanish towards them.

Pop pulled both of his pistols from his hip and ordered their silence so Gigi could speak. After the men complied, he stepped to the side and let her have the floor.

"I'm not here to bullshit around with either of you. This is not a robbery, nor am I here to kill any of you unless I don't get what I came here for."

"Fuck you, Gianna, you stupid bitch, you could've been a part of this familia, but you chose to leave, so fuck you and what you came here for, bitch. Death is an honorable salutation over betrayal," one of the men stated before settling back against his restraints.

"Your choice, idiot." Gigi didn't hesitate to blow his head off.

The round entered his left eye socket and blew a large portion of brain and skull against the wall behind him and drenched his partner next to him.

"Raul, what will it be?" Gigi asked the last living person. She hoped that he'd be smarter than his friend.

"What is it that you want of me?" he asked her in Spanish and she replied in the same.

"Who gave the order to have me followed and who ordered the hit?"

"Gianna, mami, you killed Emilia at her home and all that lived with her. They have it all on camera footage because you neglected to execute how you were trained. It's no one's fault that you killed your own sister over money but your own, and why would you even think that nothing was gonna follow that?" This time he spoke in English to emphasize the effect of his words.

Pop and Monsta both looked to her in bewilderment. There was no amount of money in the world that could make them turn on each other. They religiously believed in loyalty over everything.

"Raul, none of that matters. All I wanna know is who called the hit on me and my people?"

Raul shook his head because she surely wasn't getting it.

"Gianna, it was all done on live footage. Have you been away that long for you to know not who runs the family?" Raul hated being in this position, but the love he had and always would have for her would stand before his own life.

"Damn," she whispered as the realization of what was to come hit her dead on. "Let's go."

"Wh——are you crazy? We're actually about to leave up outta here with him still living?" Monsta retorted.

"He won't say anything to bring harm to me," she explained.

"And why the hell not?" Monsta went on.

"He's my brother," Gianna replied, shocking both Monsta and Pop.

"You have my word that I'll clean this up. Just keep her safe, because he's already coming after all of you," Raul stated.

Everyone's attention and weapons turned towards the unmistakable sound of someone's hands clapping together.

"That was a nice performance you put on," Young Mack spoke as he made himself seen, followed by a seven-man hit squad.

"You," Monsta said, while ice-grilling the opposition.

"Yeah, me, nigga, who else can I be?" Young Mack replied. "Anyways, Gianna, is it?" he asked, stepping past the hulking smaller half of the two brothers.

"What is it to you, and what the hell you doing here?"

After looking around the bloodied room and at the three dead lying around the place, he looked back into her strong, dark eyes.

"I'm here to kill him, and I would say the rest of them, but you've done a pretty good job of that already. Only unlike you, I already know who I'm after and everything that resembles their brand."

The reality that these men were here to kill her brother was almost enough to make her feel some type of way. Almost.

"But after hearing that he's your brother and you don't wanna see him dead as well as him not wanting to see you harmed, I figured maybe, just maybe, you could convince him to give me everything stored here that you were about to leave here without." Young Mack stood only inches away from the tattooed beauty. He was so close to her that she could smell the big red bubble gum mixed with the cognac on his breath.

Gianna looked to her brother and saw the surprise in his eyes as he stared up at the man before her that he'd never laid eyes on before, wondering how anyone outside of their familia could know anything about what was stored there.

"What if he chooses his loyalty over all else?"

"I'm sure that won't be the case," Young Mack assured her just as a red beam zoned in on her forehead, and once he stood to her side, they were seen all over her body.

"No, it shall not come to that," Raul spoke out.

"Good man." Young Mack smiled.

$ $ $ $ $

"This shit is crazy," Agent Drexler said with his mouth filled with apple cinnamon bear claw.

"Yeah, tell me about it," Agent Chandler added as he, too, looked over the dead bodies sprawled out and covered with bloodstained white sheets.

"I want whoever's responsible for this locked up and thrown away for the rest of their miserable lives!" they heard the Director yell at other members of the Bureau.

"He's surely pissed," Drexler spoke again with his mouth full.

"What's new?" Chandler nonchalantly moved around the place, not really caring what took place there. His intuition told him something bigger was amiss on this entire death trail. He noted that all the deceased were equipped with automatic assault rifles nearby.

He watched carefully and monitored everything and everyone their Director came in contact with. His movements had been especially suspicious ever since Mackentosh Miller warned him of all things not being as they may seem, and now things were becoming a bit clearer in his eyes. He was accustomed to the arrogant egoism which his supervisor exuded most times, and even his slight racism was expected. One thing that he'd never get used to was his bosses over-exaggerated concern with crime scenes. His suspicions were rising above a peak until they were blown flat outta space like a satellite leaving earth in a rocket by NASA.

"Excuse me, sir, what are you doing in here?" Chandler spooked Director Gamble.

"Ah ,fuck, you scared me, you nosy son of a bitch." Gamble sighed while carefully holding something in his palm so that Chandler couldn't see it.

"I mean, if I weren't the agent that I am, I would easily think that you touching anything in this room or anything in this entire place would be considered tampering." Chandler leaned up against the frame of the door.

"You silly piece of shit. I'm your superior, not your partner or anyone beneath you, so if you could touch shit and be Dick Tracey around this mutherfucker, what exactly makes you think that I can't?" Director Gamble shot back. He'd never admit it, but everything about Agent Chandler made him nervous, and now was no different as sweat began to bead his forehead in the cold factory setting.

"You mean besides the fact that you're not wearing gloves and you're standing there sweating as if it's one hundred degrees in here when this place is near freezing?"

"You think you know everything, don't you? Well, you're nothing but a black burnt up piece of shit coming up in here harassing me about PPE when there's nearly a dozen dead bodies lying around here," Director Gamble grumbled as he reached inside of his pocket and removed a pair of latex gloves, putting them on as he exited the surveillance room.

Agent Chandler stepped closer to the one monitor that still seemed to be working and read the messages that assured his suspicious and proved his new ally to be dead on about the crooked man he called his superior. The evidence sat before his eyes in a message reading, "memory deleted".

"Son of a bitch!" Chandler growled before clenching his fists.

"You should've stayed outta this, Chandler."

He jerked his body around and locked eyes with the one person he thought would have had his back through thick and thin.

"What are you doing?" Chandler questioned as he raised both hands at shoulder level in surrender.

"I've tried hard as I possibly could to keep you from jumping into the lion's mouth, but you are one persistent bastard."

"Wait, think about this for a second, man. You don't want me on your conscience like this. You're a better man than that," Chandler tried buying himself some time.

"Wow, that was classic, but not accurate at all. You see, I told the big wigs that you were gonna be a problem for our cause, and like always, I was right. Just like my last partner, you didn't let me down one bit, and that alone proves me worthy of something. Now I hate that it's come to this, but we'd be dumb not to swat the fly that infected the country with a virus," Agent Drexler stated as he screwed the silencer on a gun that was too familiar to Chandler. He reached to his side and noticed that he had indeed left his service weapon inside their car.

"So you're gonna kill me, all for your so-called cause?" Chandler nervously questioned his partner.

"Hey, I don't make the calls. I just step up where I'm needed," Drexler stated while looking him directly in the eyes.

"You muthafuc——" Chandler yelled, but got cut short from the single round to his chest. He stumbled back and fell over a fire extinguisher on his back.

Drexler stepped closer and looked down on him before emptying the clip in his body and leaving out as quietly as he came, closing the door behind him.

Chapter 15

"That's four with one more to go," Mackmillions stated after breaking the neck of the last guard inside the Realm's second to last remaining Houston stash house.

"Yeah, that's four alright," KenKen agreed with a solemn expression.

"Why the long face? Don't tell me you're starting to have regrets." Max chambered a round in the head of his weapon after hearing this.

"Man, would you chill out with the theatrics already!" KenKen mugged Max, who just looked back at him with his usual deadly stare. "What I was referring to was that the only spot left for us to take down is that of the Governors. It'll be a death trap if we go at it alone with how heavily guarded that place is. He has both law enforcement and Realm security around him like clockwork, and by now I'm sure they already know we're coming," KenKen explained his concern with their next mission.

"All of that may be true, but I'm not letting these suckas make it until I have back what's mine in full." Mackmillions knew the last post would be tough, but what other way to bring the king from his throne than to take his riches and bring him looking for you?

"Not a ting is too much fa us," Max spoke up, and he rarely did that.

"Well, what do you have in mind, Max?"

189

$$$$$

The night air was calm and the sky was clear with stars shining clear all over space. Governor Michael Robouk sat outside of his luxurious mansion watching the scantily-clad beauties play in his meter pool. Little to no people knew about this spot he frequented so often when it was hot in the streets or when there was too much politics surrounding his job. He loved the peaceful and quiet getaways his connections to the underworld provided for him with tonight being no different. He wasn't the least bit shocked when the trio of mixed-breed young beauties showed up at his front door being escorted by one of their own.

"Nice night tonight, am I right?" The Governor smiled as he raised his glass to the giddy females who waved their tops above their heads in laughter.

"No doubt about it," KenKen replied as he removed an expensive bottle of aged bourbon from a bucket of ice. He was still unsure of how he'd once again let the fellas convince him of being bait in this big pool of sharks.

"So, have you heard about the hits on our Houston locations yet?" the Governor asked, shocking KenKen with the question.

"I've heard a few rumors here and there, but nothing exclusive enough for me to believe any of it," KenKen replied while keeping a stone face.

"Well, you better believe it, because it's certainly true." The Governor stood from his seat and shook away his Versace house coat to reveal what looked like a natural coat made of dark hair all over his upper body. "Let's take a dip with these ladies for a while. You look like you could use it." The Governor smiled and ran for the pool before leaping into the air like a kid and making a big splash.

"Fuck it," KenKen said to himself, knowing it'd be best if he stayed in character and acted his part.

Once he made it to the pool's edge, he could see the Governor making out with one of the women while another serviced him under water. *It's gonna be a long night*, KenKen thought to himself as he slid into the water and motioned for the unoccupied women to come to him.

"Damn, I'm glad you decided to join in, because I'd hate to waste these talents on such short notes," the brown-skinned bombshell whispered in his ear before biting his earlobe.

"Let me check you out then, sweetheart," KenKen replied with his hands pushing down on her shoulders.

"Yes, I just gotta have some of this big monster," she replied while gripping his muscle as she descended underwater and wrapped her lips around the head of his dick.

KenKen gasped as her lips made contact with him and at the same time, he felt a tight constriction compress around his throat. He kicked his feet wildly as the oxygen was snatched from his body immediately, causing his eyes to bulge out. He reached desperately for the rope that coiled his neck as it grew tighter and tighter, causing his vision to blur. His head suddenly began to throb and his tongue swelled while his face and lips began discoloring.

Pwww! Pwww! Pwww!

Max sent three successive hollows, silenced by the suppressor he took his time screwing onto his weapon, through the coward's skull.

KenKen felt the warm splatter of liquid slick the back of his head and neck followed by the release of pressure on his neck. He fought hard to breathe and was rewarded with tasteful oxygen. Governor Robouk flinched hard after witnessing his security guard's head explode. Both women were underwater, taking turns topping him off and kissing each other, and were oblivious to what was going on.

"Stop! Get up, bitches, I'm not trying to die tonight!" He shoved them away before turning to climb out of the pool.

Their protests fell on deaf ears as he quickly made his way back inside his home. Just when he began to feel a bit safe, all the lights on the property went out, scaring the shit outta him. He locked the patio doors and made his way into the kitchen.

"You chose the wrong side, Michael," a deep baritone could be heard coming from the entertainment room opposite of the kitchen.

"Who's there? Do you know who I am? You'll never see the light of day again if something happens to me. Just take what you came for and go. I don't know your identity, so I won't pursue this." Michael Robouk fidgeted around in his kitchen in search of something, anything, he could defend himself with.

"I certainly do plan to leave after I get all that I came here for."

As if on cue, all the lights came back on, and Michael witnessed the bloody bodies of his security detail piled atop of each other right outside the floor to ceiling windows. Max and KenKen stood with their murder weapons drenched and dripping with thick drops of blood from their victims.

"Holy shit," the Governor gasped and jumped back after noticing the three dead women he'd summoned over that were barely legal by any standards.

"You betrayed me in the worst way, Michael, and for what? A promotion that you were already in line to receive? You know, the funniest thing about it all is that I wouldn't ever imagine it be you of all people."

"You-you-you don't understand…"

"Understand what? That you snaked me for a spot in the light? Fuck is there to understand about that?" Mackmillions moved swiftly from his seat to the bar in the kitchen.

"He-he's got me by the balls, Mack. There was nothing I could do to stop him," the Governor tried to explain, but Mackmillions wasn't there for it.

"No one knew about the mission but you, and you sent them after me when you could've come to me."

"But——"

"You think I don't know all about your perverted ways and the shit you and your blood family does to every underaged girl in your family? There's all kind of shit I could've turned my back on you over, yet I remained loyal to you and your position." Mackmillions laughed at the bugged-out expression worn by the Governor. "You really didn't think that I knew all about that, did you? Never mind that though, because I have two options for you here tonight, Michael, and to be brutally honest with you, neither one of them ends without me taking your life."

Mackmillions took his gun from his hip and motioned for the Governor to open the glass patio doors for Max and KenKen. The Governor couldn't help but to stare at the pile of dead bodies as rigor mortis set in and he pictured himself lying there and staring back at himself with dead, soulless eyes. The Governor stepped back as Mackmillions' men stepped into the kitchen with death still deep in their eyes, and he knew then that they had come to kill and their mission was nearly complete.

"First option I have for you, Michael, is that you could help yourself by telling me everything I need to know about the muthafucka I'm after, which would bring you a painless death." Mackmillions set his gun on the bar top for emphasis. "Option two would be allowing my men to torture you by cutting your body into pieces while you're still alive to feel every single piece of you being removed," Mackmillions concluded.

"Fuck him, let's just cut his ass up for fun and get these answers from elsewhere. Pervert tried to have me killed," KenKen raged after a brief silence.

"No, I'll tell you everything. Just make my death easy. But no face shots so that my family could see me off," the Governor quickly agreed to comply.

"I'm listening," Mackmillions said, and paid close attention to every detail as the Governor gave him everything he needed to behead the snake of a leader of the new Realm. He even told them about the millions in cash stashed there in his wine cellar in the basement.

"I knew I'd find you here." A familiar voice got everyone's attention, and weapons pointed in the directions it came from. A chuckle left Blackwell's mouth as he entered the kitchen flanked by eight of his most trusted henchmen. "It pains me to know how much of a coward you are, Michael, but I shouldn't be shocked. After all, look at how you turned your back on Mr. Mack here. There is no amount of dignity left in your miserable body, you sorry excuse of a human. And you...I've been wanting to get my hands on you for so long that I can nearly taste the stench of your death. Damn, how delightful! I knew it would be when that time finally came," Blackwell stated with his eyes closed as if in a trance before opening them to look Mackmillions directly in his.

"We both know how this is gonna end, so why don't you do us both a favor and tell your men to step off now to save their lives later."

Mackmillions kept his game face on while never taking his weapon off of his targeted enemy.

"I believe we're reading from two different books, Miller. See, where you show mercy and sometimes compassion, I don't," Blackwell said before blowing a colossal chunk of the Governor's face off. The impact was so strong that it threw the Governor's body up against the wall, where his brain and bone fragments decorated it. "Pussy!"

"The way I see it is, now you have one of two options, Miller."

"Oh yeah? And what are those? Humor me." Mackmillions knew he had to play this thing carefully because as bad as he wanted to put a round into Blackwell's face like he'd just done the Governor, he wasn't tryna die in the process of it all.

"First, we can start by you putting those weapons down because you're smart enough to know that you're outnumbered and out weaponed. Then we could kick this off by you telling me where I can find all of the money you took from me and maybe, just maybe, I'd feel inclined to allow you to come and work for me after every dime is returned."

Mackmillions chuckled, and his reflex nearly made him pull the trigger on this phony bad boy.

"Or secondly, you could choose to die right here right now," Blackwell stated with venom from the direct disrespect, but he didn't dare raise his weapon because Mackmillions already had him in his line of fire.

Mackmillions shook his head at the egomaniac standing before him. Max, on the other hand, was secretly plotting their escape when he locked eyes with KenKen, who noticed the wheels turning in his head, conjuring up an outrageous plot. Mackmillions heard the familiar sound of pin disconnecting from its registered place as Max used to love doing that years ago from there. He knew it was time to giddy up outta there.

"You really don't understand who you're dealing with do you, bad ass?" Mackmillions lowered his weapon to his lap with the business end facing the obviously trigger-happy goons Blackwell had posted there blocking the entrance to the entertainment room.

"Is that your choice?" Blackwell felt pressured and for some reason nervous.

"I'll be at you soon real soon," Mackmillions stated before Max tossed the single grenade over the island in the path of Blackwell's only escape from the kitchen.

Mackmillions fired rapidly, connecting with three of the eight men. KenKen blasted, providing cover for Max, who turned away while grabbing Mackmillions by his shirt collar, pulling him to cover. The deafening sound of the explosion made their ears ring from being so close to the blast. Shots were sent in their direction, but they were up and on their feet and out the front door, barely escaping with their lives.

$ $ $ $ $

Agent Chandler's mind raced, glancing back at all that he'd ever been through. Nothing could ever compare to the amount of betrayal he felt at the moment. The pain from his wounds was numbing, but the mounting anger deep inside fueled him more now than ever, burning deep, worse than the rounds that connected with his service vest. The pain from his side where he felt something that he hadn't felt in ages alerted him to the wetness beneath him. He was hit, but remained motionless. Braving the torture of the pregnant silence nearly sent his nerves in shock. For an entire hour he laid still before fishing his iPhone from his pocket. His straining eyes roamed the brightness of the gadget's screen. His battery was nearing its life's end, but it managed to hold and was undoubtedly a true lifesaver.

"Yello!" Chandler heard the high-pitched sound of his friend's voice.

"I'm hurt, Kirk."

"Ced?"

"Yeah, track my location, come alone. I'm stranded and I'm hurt bad," Chandler weakly replied.

"Ced, hold on, buddy, I'm on my way!"

$ $ $ $ $

"Fuck, he's finished! I want that black fuck squashed immediately! I want every fucking available street thug and hired hitmen on the prowl for his head right now!" Blackwell yelled through the antagonizing pain of his burns.

The grenade blast managed to scorch the entire right side of his face and body. Max was indeed strategic with his plan to escape death's clutch on them in that crowded kitchen. His actions not only saved their lives, but they also crucially altered that of Blackwell's and his surviving men.

"I want a twenty-four-hour manhunt for this mutherfucker and his men. I want to hunt down and skin every member of his fucking family while they're still alive. What-what the hell is that?" Blackwell detoured from his rant when he felt a sudden wetness trickle down the back of neck.

He turned back in his seat and his eyes nearly bugged outta his head as he stared at the gruesome sight of his headless men in the backseat. His voice completely escaped him as he watched in fear as his driver's head got ripped from his neck effortlessly before the vehicle collided with the freeway's medium of their Holister exit. Blackwell's head hurt tremendously from the metal clashing with the hulking concrete. His vision was completely blurred, but his senses remain intact, and he sensed his life was in immediate danger. He reached beside his body and released his seatbelt, then pulled on the door's release. Spilling out of the SUV and onto the deserted freeway's off ramp, Blackwell reached for his side weapon and fired wildly at the windows of the truck, hoping to kill the hideous thing inside. He'd never in life witnessed the strength of the thing that destroyed his men inside their truck. That thing had majestical stealth and immense power, and he wanted no parts of it. He scrambled to his feet, but stumbled quickly as he tried to distance himself from the death that loomed behind him. Just as hope began to set in, a sharp, excruciating pain burst throughout his entire body, and it felt as if he'd been hit in the kidney with a solid baseball bat. An overpowering fright kept his feet moving before mobility left his limbs. Stuck there in shock, Blackwell's eyes fell upon the death bringer himself. His eyes were like nothing that Blackwell had ever witnessed. The sharp teeth and scaled skin sent him on a whirlwind between mental insanity and immediate reality.

The deadly smirk on the thing's face rendered Blackwell inaudible in his desperate plea for mercy.

Gator took pride in his work and was happy to appease the direct threat on his family. He smiled joyously while unraveling Blackwell's intestines before using them to suspend his body from the overhang of the freeway for the early morning traffic to find.

$ $ $ $ $

"Bruh, we gotta get the fuck outta Dodge!" KenKen stated in a state of clear panic. "He knows I'm with the shits, he seen me with his own two eyes, bodies piled outside, smoking gun in hand. Man, he gon' kill my girl, did y'all see how he blew the Governor's head off? Mack, you gotta tell me where you're keeping her. I've proved my worth and loyalty, and I want her back. Mack, I need to get my girl and get ghost. I'm talking new identities…"

"Can I shoot him now?" Max cut in as KenKen rambled restlessly.

"Both of y'all calm down for a bit," Mackmillions stated in his always calm, deep baritone.

KenKen couldn't understand how neither of them weren't panic stricken just as he was. They had barely escaped Blackwell's death trap and now he had seen him. His cover was blown now and shit was about to get really real for them and their loved ones.

"Mack, you got a wife and kid. How are you not worried about shit spiraling out of control? We're blown. It's a wrap!" KenKen made animated hand gestures while he explained their predicament in detail.

"First, your woman is fine. She's at her sister's house, whose husband happens to be a near and dear friend of mine, and I trust him with her life to keep her safe, so she's good. Secondly, yes, I do have a wife and son, who just so happens to have his own set of problems right now, and I'm sure just like his pops, they're being taken care of." Mackmillions paused as he came to a stop with KenKen's full attention now on their surroundings.

"Mack, I fucks with you hard, but seriously, man, what the fuck are we doing here?"

"Third and most importantly, right about now..." Mackmillions looked at the time on his Swiss Chronograph before continuing. "Blackwell is a non-issue." He smiled.

KenKen followed his eyes through the thick darkness and watched as something approached. Something big – no, not something, but someone. And as the figure closed in on them, KenKen couldn't believe his eyes.

"What the fuck is that?"

To Be Continued...

P.O.T.S. 3
Coming Soon

Lock Down Publications and Ca$h Presents
Assisted Publishing Packages

BASIC PACKAGE $499 Editing Cover Design Formatting	UPGRADED PACKAGE $800 Typing Editing Cover Design Formatting
ADVANCE PACKAGE $1,200 Typing Editing Cover Design Formatting Copyright registration Proofreading Upload book to Amazon	LDP SUPREME PACKAGE $1,500 Typing Editing Cover Design Formatting Copyright registration Proofreading Set up Amazon account Upload book to Amazon Advertise on LDP, Amazon and Facebook Page

***Other services available upon request.
Additional charges may apply

Lock Down Publications
P.O. Box 944
Stockbridge, GA 30281-9998
Phone: 470 303-9761

Submission Guideline

Submit the first three chapters of your completed manuscript to ldpsubmissions@gmail.com. In the subject line add **Your Book's Title**. The manuscript must be in a Word Doc file and sent as an attachment. Document should be in Times New Roman, double spaced, and in size 12 font. Also, provide your synopsis and full contact information. If sending multiple submissions, they must each be in a separate email.

Have a story but no way to send it electronically? You can still submit to LDP/Ca$h Presents. Send in the first three chapters, written or typed, of your completed manuscript to:

LDP: Submissions Dept
P.O. Box 944
Stockbridge, GA 30281-9998

DO NOT send original manuscript. Must be a duplicate. Provide your synopsis and a cover letter containing your full contact information.

Thanks for considering LDP and Ca$h Presents.

NEW RELEASES

BLOODLINE OF A SAVAGE **BY PRINCE A. TAUHID**

THE MURDER QUEENS 4 **BY MICHAEL GALLON**

THE BUTTERFLY MAFIA **BY FUMIYA PAYNE**

KING KILLA 2 **BY VINCENT "VITTO" HOLLOWAY**

BABY, I'M WINTERTIME COLD 3 **BY MEESHA**

THESE VICIOUS STREETS **BY PRINCE A. TAUHID**

TIL DEATH 2 **BY ARYANNA**

CITY OF SMOKE 2 **BY MOLOTTI**

STEPPERS **BY KING RIO**

THE LANE **BY KEN-KEN SPENCE**

MONEY GAME 2 **BY SMOOVE DOLLA**

THE BLACK DIAMOND CARTEL **BY SAYNOMORE**

CRIME BOSS 2 **BY PLAYA RAY**

THUG OF SPADES **BY COREY ROBINSON**

LOVE IN THE TRENCHES 2 **BY COREY ROBINSON**

TIL DEATH 3 **BY ARYANNA**

THE BIRTH OF A GANGSTER 4 **BY DELMONT PLAYER**

PRODUCT OF THE STREETS **BY DEMOND "MONEY" ANDERSON**

Coming Soon from Lock Down Publications/Ca$h Presents

BLOOD OF A BOSS VI
SHADOWS OF THE GAME II
TRAP BASTARD II
By **Askari**

LOYAL TO THE GAME IV
By **T.J. & Jelissa**

TRUE SAVAGE VIII
MIDNIGHT CARTEL IV
DOPE BOY MAGIC IV
CITY OF KINGZ III
NIGHTMARE ON SILENT AVE II
THE PLUG OF LIL MEXICO II
CLASSIC CITY II
By **Chris Green**

BLAST FOR ME III
A SAVAGE DOPEBOY III
CUTTHROAT MAFIA III
DUFFLE BAG CARTEL VII
HEARTLESS GOON VI
By **Ghost**

A HUSTLER'S DECEIT III
KILL ZONE II
BAE BELONGS TO ME III
TIL DEATH II
By **Aryanna**

KING OF THE TRAP III
By **T.J. Edwards**

GORILLAZ IN THE BAY V
3X KRAZY III
STRAIGHT BEAST MODE III
By **De'Kari**

KINGPIN KILLAZ IV
STREET KINGS III
PAID IN BLOOD III
CARTEL KILLAZ IV
DOPE GODS III
By **Hood Rich**

SINS OF A HUSTLA II
By **ASAD**

YAYO V
BRED IN THE GAME 2
By **S. Allen**

THE STREETS WILL TALK II
By **Yolanda Moore**

SON OF A DOPE FIEND III
HEAVEN GOT A GHETTO III
SKI MASK MONEY III
By **Renta**

LOYALTY AIN'T PROMISED III
By **Keith Williams**

I'M NOTHING WITHOUT HIS LOVE II
SINS OF A THUG II
TO THE THUG I LOVED BEFORE II
IN A HUSTLER I TRUST II
By **Monet Dragun**

QUIET MONEY IV
EXTENDED CLIP III
THUG LIFE IV
By **Trai'Quan**

THE STREETS MADE ME IV
By **Larry D. Wright**

IF YOU CROSS ME ONCE III
ANGEL V
By **Anthony Fields**

THE STREETS WILL NEVER CLOSE IV
By **K'ajji**

HARD AND RUTHLESS III
KILLA KOUNTY IV
By **Khufu**

MONEY GAME III
By **Smoove Dolla**

MURDA WAS THE CASE III
Elijah R. Freeman

AN UNFORESEEN LOVE IV
BABY, I'M WINTERTIME COLD III
By **Meesha**

QUEEN OF THE ZOO III
By **Black Migo**

CONFESSIONS OF A JACKBOY III
By **Nicholas Lock**

JACK BOYS VS DOPE BOYS IV
A GANGSTA'S QUR'AN V
COKE GIRLZ II
COKE BOYS II
LIFE OF A SAVAGE V
CHI'RAQ GANGSTAS V
SOSA GANG III
BRONX SAVAGES II
BODYMORE KINGPINS II
By **Romell Tukes**

KING KILLA II
By **Vincent "Vitto" Holloway**

BETRAYAL OF A THUG III
By **Fre$h**

THE MURDER QUEENS III
By **Michael Gallon**

THE BIRTH OF A GANGSTER III
By **Delmont Player**

TREAL LOVE II
By **Le'Monica Jackson**

FOR THE LOVE OF BLOOD III
By **Jamel Mitchell**

RAN OFF ON DA PLUG II
By **Paper Boi Rari**

HOOD CONSIGLIERE III
By **Keese**

PRETTY GIRLS DO NASTY THINGS II
By **Nicole Goosby**

PROTÉGÉ OF A LEGEND III
LOVE IN THE TRENCHES II
By **Corey Robinson**

IT'S JUST ME AND YOU II
By **Ah'Million**

FOREVER GANGSTA III
By **Adrian Dulan**

GORILLAZ IN THE TRENCHES II
By **SayNoMore**

THE COCAINE PRINCESS VIII
By **King Rio**

CRIME BOSS II
By **Playa Ray**

LOYALTY IS EVERYTHING III
By **Molotti**

HERE TODAY GONE TOMORROW II
By **Fly Rock**

REAL G'S MOVE IN SILENCE II
By **Von Diesel**

GRIMEY WAYS IV
By **Ray Vinci**

Available Now

RESTRAINING ORDER I & II
By **CA$H & Coffee**

LOVE KNOWS NO BOUNDARIES I II & III
By **Coffee**

RAISED AS A GOON I, II, III & IV
BRED BY THE SLUMS I, II, III
BLAST FOR ME I & II
ROTTEN TO THE CORE I II III
A BRONX TALE I, II, III
DUFFLE BAG CARTEL I II III IV V VI
HEARTLESS GOON I II III IV V
A SAVAGE DOPEBOY I II
DRUG LORDS I II III
CUTTHROAT MAFIA I II
KING OF THE TRENCHES
By **Ghost**

LAY IT DOWN I & II
LAST OF A DYING BREED I II
BLOOD STAINS OF A SHOTTA I & II III
By **Jamaica**

LOYAL TO THE GAME I II III
LIFE OF SIN I, II III
By **TJ & Jelissa**

IF LOVING HIM IS WRONG…I & II
LOVE ME EVEN WHEN IT HURTS I II III
By **Jelissa**

BLOODY COMMAS I & II
SKI MASK CARTEL I, II & III
KING OF NEW YORK I II, III IV V
RISE TO POWER I II III
COKE KINGS I II III IV V
BORN HEARTLESS I II III IV
KING OF THE TRAP I II
By **T.J. Edwards**

WHEN THE STREETS CLAP BACK I & II III
THE HEART OF A SAVAGE I II III IV
MONEY MAFIA I II
LOYAL TO THE SOIL I II III
By **Jibril Williams**

A DISTINGUISHED THUG STOLE MY HEART I II &
III
LOVE SHOULDN'T HURT I II III IV
RENEGADE BOYS I II III IV
PAID IN KARMA I II III
SAVAGE STORMS I II III
AN UNFORESEEN LOVE I II III
BABY, I'M WINTERTIME COLD I II
By **Meesha**

A GANGSTER'S CODE I &, II III
A GANGSTER'S SYN I II III
THE SAVAGE LIFE I II III
CHAINED TO THE STREETS I II III
BLOOD ON THE MONEY I II III
A GANGSTA'S PAIN I II III
By **J-Blunt**

PUSH IT TO THE LIMIT
By **Bre' Hayes**

BLOOD OF A BOSS I, II, III, IV, V
SHADOWS OF THE GAME
TRAP BASTARD
By **Askari**

THE STREETS BLEED MURDER I, II & III
THE HEART OF A GANGSTA I II& III
By **Jerry Jackson**

CUM FOR ME I II III IV V VI VII VIII
An **LDP Erotica Collaboration**

BRIDE OF A HUSTLA I II & II
THE FETTI GIRLS I, II& III
CORRUPTED BY A GANGSTA I, II III, IV
BLINDED BY HIS LOVE
THE PRICE YOU PAY FOR LOVE I, II ,III
DOPE GIRL MAGIC I II III
By **Destiny Skai**

WHEN A GOOD GIRL GOES BAD
By **Adrienne**

A GANGSTER'S REVENGE I II III & IV
THE BOSS MAN'S DAUGHTERS I II III IV V
A SAVAGE LOVE I & II
BAE BELONGS TO ME I II
A HUSTLER'S DECEIT I, II, III
WHAT BAD BITCHES DO I, II, III
SOUL OF A MONSTER I II III
KILL ZONE
A DOPE BOY'S QUEEN I II III
TIL DEATH
By **Aryanna**

THE COST OF LOYALTY I II III
By Kweli

A KINGPIN'S AMBITION
A KINGPIN'S AMBITION **II**
I MURDER FOR THE DOUGH
By **Ambitious**

TRUE SAVAGE I II III IV V VI VII
DOPE BOY MAGIC I, II, III
MIDNIGHT CARTEL I II III
CITY OF KINGZ I II
NIGHTMARE ON SILENT AVE
THE PLUG OF LIL MEXICO II
CLASSIC CITY
By **Chris Green**

A DOPEBOY'S PRAYER
By **Eddie "Wolf" Lee**

THE KING CARTEL I, II & III
By **Frank Gresham**

THESE NIGGAS AIN'T LOYAL I, II & III
By **Nikki Tee**

GANGSTA SHYT I II &III
By **CATO**

THE ULTIMATE BETRAYAL
By **Phoenix**

BOSS'N UP I, II & III
By **Royal Nicole**

I LOVE YOU TO DEATH
By **Destiny J**

I RIDE FOR MY HITTA
I STILL RIDE FOR MY HITTA
By **Misty Holt**

LOVE & CHASIN' PAPER
By **Qay Crockett**

TO DIE IN VAIN
SINS OF A HUSTLA
By **ASAD**

BROOKLYN HUSTLAZ
By **Boogsy Morina**

BROOKLYN ON LOCK I & II
By **Sonovia**

GANGSTA CITY
By **Teddy Duke**

A DRUG KING AND HIS DIAMOND I & II III
A DOPEMAN'S RICHES
HER MAN, MINE'S TOO I, II
CASH MONEY HO'S
THE WIFEY I USED TO BE I II
PRETTY GIRLS DO NASTY THINGS
By Nicole Goosby

LIPSTICK KILLAH I, II, III
CRIME OF PASSION I II & III
FRIEND OR FOE I II III
By **Mimi**

TRAPHOUSE KING I II & III
KINGPIN KILLAZ I II III
STREET KINGS I II
PAID IN BLOOD I II
CARTEL KILLAZ I II III
DOPE GODS I II
By **Hood Rich**

STEADY MOBBN' I, II, III
THE STREETS STAINED MY SOUL I II III
By **Marcellus Allen**

WHO SHOT YA I, II, III
SON OF A DOPE FIEND I II
HEAVEN GOT A GHETTO I II
SKI MASK MONEY I II
By **Renta**

GORILLAZ IN THE BAY I II III IV
TEARS OF A GANGSTA I II
3X KRAZY I II
STRAIGHT BEAST MODE I II
By **DE'KARI**

TRIGGADALE I II III
MURDA WAS THE CASE I II
By **Elijah R. Freeman**

THE STREETS ARE CALLING
By **Duquie Wilson**

SLAUGHTER GANG I II III
RUTHLESS HEART I II III
By **Willie Slaughter**

GOD BLESS THE TRAPPERS I, II, III
THESE SCANDALOUS STREETS I, II, III
FEAR MY GANGSTA I, II, III IV, V
THESE STREETS DON'T LOVE NOBODY I, II
BURY ME A G I, II, III, IV, V
A GANGSTA'S EMPIRE I, II, III, IV
THE DOPEMAN'S BODYGAURD I II
THE REALEST KILLAZ I II III
THE LAST OF THE OGS I II III
By **Tranay Adams**

MARRIED TO A BOSS I II III
By **Destiny Skai & Chris Green**

KINGZ OF THE GAME I II III IV V VI VII
CRIME BOSS
By **Playa Ray**

FUK SHYT
By **Blakk Diamond**

DON'T F#CK WITH MY HEART I II
By **Linnea**

ADDICTED TO THE DRAMA I II III
IN THE ARM OF HIS BOSS II
By **Jamila**

YAYO I II III IV
A SHOOTER'S AMBITION I II
BRED IN THE GAME
By **S. Allen**

LOYALTY AIN'T PROMISED I II
By **Keith Williams**

TRAP GOD I II III
RICH $AVAGE I II III
MONEY IN THE GRAVE I II III
By **Martell Troublesome Bolden**

FOREVER GANGSTA I II
GLOCKS ON SATIN SHEETS I II
By **Adrian Dulan**

TOE TAGZ I II III IV
LEVELS TO THIS SHYT I II
IT'S JUST ME AND YOU
By **Ah'Million**

KINGPIN DREAMS I II III
RAN OFF ON DA PLUG
By **Paper Boi Rari**

CONFESSIONS OF A GANGSTA I II III IV
CONFESSIONS OF A JACKBOY I II
By **Nicholas Lock**

I'M NOTHING WITHOUT HIS LOVE
SINS OF A THUG
TO THE THUG I LOVED BEFORE
A GANGSTA SAVED XMAS
IN A HUSTLER I TRUST
By **Monet Dragun**

QUIET MONEY I II III
THUG LIFE I II III
EXTENDED CLIP I II
A GANGSTA'S PARADISE
By **Trai'Quan**

CAUGHT UP IN THE LIFE I II III
THE STREETS NEVER LET GO I II III
By **Robert Baptiste**

NEW TO THE GAME I II III
MONEY, MURDER & MEMORIES I II III
By **Malik D. Rice**

CREAM I II III
THE STREETS WILL TALK
By **Yolanda Moore**

LIFE OF A SAVAGE I II III IV
A GANGSTA'S QUR'AN I II III IV
MURDA SEASON I II III
GANGLAND CARTEL I II III
CHI'RAQ GANGSTAS I II III IV
KILLERS ON ELM STREET I II III
JACK BOYZ N DA BRONX I II III
A DOPEBOY'S DREAM I II III
JACK BOYS VS DOPE BOYS I II III
COKE GIRLZ
COKE BOYS
SOSA GANG I II
BRONX SAVAGES
BODYMORE KINGPINS
By **Romell Tukes**

THE STREETS MADE ME I II III
By **Larry D. Wright**

CONCRETE KILLA I II III
VICIOUS LOYALTY I II III
By **Kingpen**

217

THE ULTIMATE SACRIFICE I, II, III, IV, V, VI
KHADIFI
IF YOU CROSS ME ONCE I II
ANGEL I II III IV
IN THE BLINK OF AN EYE
By **Anthony Fields**

THE LIFE OF A HOOD STAR
By **Ca$h & Rashia Wilson**

THE STREETS WILL NEVER CLOSE I II III
By **K'ajji**

NIGHTMARES OF A HUSTLA I II III
By **King Dream**

HARD AND RUTHLESS I II
MOB TOWN 251
THE BILLIONAIRE BENTLEYS I II III
REAL G'S MOVE IN SILENCE
By **Von Diesel**

GHOST MOB
By **Stilloan Robinson**

MOB TIES I II III IV V VI
SOUL OF A HUSTLER, HEART OF A KILLER I II
GORILLAZ IN THE TRENCHES
By **SayNoMore**

BODYMORE MURDERLAND I II III
THE BIRTH OF A GANGSTER I II
By **Delmont Player**

FOR THE LOVE OF A BOSS
By **C. D. Blue**

KILLA KOUNTY I II III IV
By Khufu

MOBBED UP I II III IV
THE BRICK MAN I II III IV V
THE COCAINE PRINCESS I II III IV V VI VII
By **King Rio**

MONEY GAME I II
By **Smoove Dolla**

A GANGSTA'S KARMA I II III
By **FLAME**

KING OF THE TRENCHES I II III
By **GHOST & TRANAY ADAMS**

QUEEN OF THE ZOO I II
By **Black Migo**

GRIMEY WAYS I II III
By **Ray Vinci**

XMAS WITH AN ATL SHOOTER
By **Ca$h & Destiny Skai**

KING KILLA
By **Vincent "Vitto" Holloway**

BETRAYAL OF A THUG I II
By **Fre$h**

THE MURDER QUEENS I II
By **Michael Gallon**

TREAL LOVE
By **Le'Monica Jackson**

FOR THE LOVE OF BLOOD I II
By **Jamel Mitchell**

HOOD CONSIGLIERE I II
By **Keese**

PROTÉGÉ OF A LEGEND I II
LOVE IN THE TRENCHES
By **Corey Robinson**

BORN IN THE GRAVE I II III
By **Self Made Tay**

MOAN IN MY MOUTH
By **XTASY**

TORN BETWEEN A GANGSTER AND A
GENTLEMAN
By **J-BLUNT & Miss Kim**

LOYALTY IS EVERYTHING I II
By **Molotti**

HERE TODAY GONE TOMORROW
By **Fly Rock**

PILLOW PRINCESS
By **S. Hawkins**

SANCTIFIED AND HORNY
by **XTASY**

THE PLUG OF LIL MEXICO 2
by **CHRIS GREEN**

THE BLACK DIAMOND CARTEL
by **SAYNOMORE**

THE BIRTH OF A GANGSTER 3
by **DELMONT PLAYER**

BOOKS BY LDP'S CEO, CA$H

TRUST IN NO MAN
TRUST IN NO MAN 2
TRUST IN NO MAN 3
BONDED BY BLOOD
SHORTY GOT A THUG
THUGS CRY
THUGS CRY 2
THUGS CRY 3
TRUST NO BITCH
TRUST NO BITCH 2
TRUST NO BITCH 3
TIL MY CASKET DROPS
RESTRAINING ORDER
RESTRAINING ORDER 2
IN LOVE WITH A CONVICT
LIFE OF A HOOD STAR
XMAS WITH AN ATL SHOOTER